THE GUNSMITH

466

Young Butch Cassidy

Books by J.R. Roberts
(Robert J. Randisi)

The Gunsmith series

Gunsmith Giant series

Lady Gunsmith series

Angel Eyes series

Tracker series

Mountain Jack Pike series

COMING SOON!
The Gunsmith
467 – The Lady Sheriff

For more information visit:
www.SpeakingVolumes.us

THE GUNSMITH

466

Young Butch Cassidy

J.R. Roberts

SPEAKING VOLUMES, LLC
NAPLES, FLORIDA
2021

Young Butch Cassidy

ISBN 978-1-64540-387-6

Chapter One

Clint Adams had never been to Columbia, Colorado before. It was in a box canyon, surrounded by cliffs and dotted with mining operations. Clint rode his Tobiano in, impressed with the way the horse had handled the mountainous trail. The two were still getting used to each other.

But he wasn't there to admire the scenery. He had been visiting his friend, John Locke, who had a ranch in Las Vegas, New Mexico, where Clint now spent some of his down time. While there, he received a telegram, sent from Denver, asking him to come to Columbia as soon as he could. It was sent by a stranger he didn't know, but on behalf of a friend of his named Benny Diamond. One of the mining operations up in the hills belonged to Benny.

Before going up into the hills to find Benny and his mine, he had to get himself situated in town in a hotel called the Columbia, get Toby taken care of, and see to the hunger pains in his belly.

It didn't take long, and soon he was seated at a table in a small cafe just a few feet from his hotel.

"What can I getcha?" the waiter asked.

"What've you got?" Clint asked.

"Anythin'," the waiter said. "You tell me what you want, and the cook will do it for ya."

"So no menu?"

"The cook doesn't like to be locked into the same dishes all the time," the middle-aged waiter said. "He likes to be challenged."

"Well, I'm easy to please," Clint said. "I need a rare steak and some vegetables."

"Comin' up!"

When the waiter brought the plate, Clint attacked it with gusto. The cook not only liked to be challenged but was excellent.

"How was that?" the waiter asked, when Clint finished.

"It was great," Clint said. "Couldn't've been better."

"Any dessert?"

"Not this time," Clint said, "but maybe you can answer some questions for me."

"Sure," the waiter said, "go ahead."

"Do the miners get down here much?"

"Some of them come down every night to blow off some steam after a hard day," the waiter said. "Some stay up there, and only come down for supplies when they need 'em."

"Do any of them eat here?"

"Once in a while," the waiter said. "There's another café at the other end of the street that feeds a lot of 'em."

"Why do they go there and not here?"

"That's easy," the waiter said. "The owner's brother is a miner."

"Ah, I see."

"We feed most of the townspeople, though, not that there are all that many. We got a couple of saloons, a general store, and a couple of other shops, but most of the people around here are miners."

"What are they mining?"

"Mostly gold," the waiter said. "Not pure, but some ore that has gold in it. That's what I hear, anyway."

"Do you know a miner named Benny Diamond?"

"Can't say I do," the waiter said, "but if you go to the other café, they know most of 'em."

"I got it," Clint said. "Okay, thanks. What do I owe you?"

He settled his bill and left the café, promising to take most of his meals there. His hotel had a small dining room that he thought he would probably use for breakfast.

He walked to the other end of the small town, found the second café. It was a little larger with a more rustic look to the walls and furniture. The tables and chair all looked handmade in a hurry.

As he entered, he saw it was as empty as the other café had been, since it was between meal times.

"Take any table," the waiter, a tall, young man said.

"I'm not here to eat," Clint said. "Somebody told me you know most of the miners, here."

"Yeah, we do," the waiter said. "My Pa's brother is a miner, my Uncle Dave."

"Would you happen to know a fella named Benny Diamond?" Clint asked.

He thought he saw recognition in the young man's eyes, but when he spoke the waiter said, "Can't say I do, Mister. But I could ask my Pa."

"I'd appreciate that."

As the boy went into the kitchen, Clint had the feeling he had been lying. When he came out, he was followed by a powerfully built man in his fifties, who looked more like a miner than a cook, except for the apron he wore. He was wiping his hands on a dirty white towel.

"You the fella askin' about Benny Diamond?"

"That's right."

"Why you want him?"

"He's a friend of mine," Clint said. "I'm looking for his operation."

"Benny's got a small claim partway up the mountain," the man said. "Most of the miners have signs up to identify their claims. Benny's says, 'Diamond's Dig.'"

"How do I get up there?"

"Well," the man said, "you can try gettin' up there, or you can wait for Benny to come down. He eats here, sometimes."

"Why'd your boy tell me he doesn't know him?"

"Because you're a stranger," the man said. "Look, I'm Felix Bourne, this is my son Jeff."

"I'm Clint Adams."

"The Gunsmith?" Jeff asked, wide-eyed. "You're friends with Benny?"

"That's right."

"Well, like I said, he'll probably come down to eat. Then he can take you back up with him, instead of you trying to find a way up there."

"Sounds like a good idea," Clint said. "Thanks for your help."

"Just stop by when you start to see the miners comin' down," Bourne advised.

"I'll do that," Clint said and left the café.

Chapter Two

Clint had a few hours before the workday ended and the miners would start coming down for supper. He decided to pay a visit to whoever the law in Columbia was. A short walk through town brought him to a small building marked SHERRIF'S OFFICE. But when he tried the door, he found it locked, he banged on it, but nobody answered. He walked to his hotel and approached the young clerk at the front desk.

"Can I help ya, Mr. Adams?" the man asked.

"Yes, you can tell me who the sheriff is, and where I might find him."

"Did you put your horse in the livery down the street?"

"I did."

"And you gave him to the hostler there?"

"An older gent with long grey hair? Yes, he was there," Clint said.

"Then you met 'im."

"Met who?" Clint asked.

"The sheriff," the clerk said.

"That old fellow?" Clint asked.

"That's Bates Monroe," the clerk said. "He's the part-time sheriff."

"Part-time?" Clint asked. "And when is that?"

"Whenever somebody needs to be put in jail," the clerk said.

"And how often is that?" Clint asked.

"Almost every night," the clerk said. "The miners come down, get liquored up, and somebody always ends up in jail."

"For how long?"

"Just until mornin'," the clerk said. "They're always let out in time to go up and work their claims."

"I see. Okay, thanks."

"Do you have a problem you need the sheriff for?" the clerk asked.

"No," Clint said, "I just like to check in with the local law when I get to a new town."

He left the hotel and headed for the livery.

***

At the livery he found the hostler sweeping up some of the dung left by the horses. He stopped to watch as Clint entered.

"Back so soon for that fine horse of yours?" he asked.

"I'm here to see the sheriff, not the hostler," Clint told him.

"That right?" the older man said. "Hold on, then." He reached into his pocket, took out what looked like a homemade tin star and pinned it on. It was both dented and tarnished, but his chest seemed to puff up proudly when he pinned it on. "There ya go. I'm Sheriff Bates Monroe. Now, what is it I can do for you?"

"I just like to check in with the law when I come to a new town," Clint said. "My name's Clint Adams."

"Adams?" the sheriff said. "The Gunsmith?"

"That's right."

"I heard you always rode a black Darley Arabian."

"Put him out to pasture, recently," Clint said. "Time for him to have a rest."

"Well," the sheriff said, "this one ain't bad."

"No, he ain't."

"What brings you to town?"

"Visiting a friend," Clint said. "Do you know Benny Diamond?"

"Sure, I know Benny."

"I was going to look for his mine, but I was advised that he might be coming down to eat tonight."

"That's possible," the sheriff said. "He does that sometimes."

"Does he keep any animals here?"

"Sure does," Monroe said. "A mule."

"I guess I'll just wait and see if he comes down, then," Clint said. "Thanks for the information, Sheriff."

"Any time."

The old man took off the badge, stuffed it back into his shirt pocket, and went on with his sweeping.

Chapter Three

Life went on outside the box canyon as well as inside.

Robert Leroy Parker drove the twelve horses ahead of him, along with his partner, Earl Foreman.

"Do you know where you're goin'?" Foreman demanded.

"Sure, I do," Parker said. "The ranch should be just over that rise."

"Should be?" Foreman asked. "You mean ya don't know? I knew I shouldn'ta let you talk me into this."

Earl Foreman was in his late thirties and had lived most of his life as a follower, not a leader. On the other hand, the twenty-year-old Parker had all the earmarks of a leader.

Parker laughed and said, "Relax, Earl, we're almost there, and that means that we're gettin' paid soon."

"You better be right," Foreman said, looking around. "The quicker we deliver the faster I can stop worryin' about bein' caught with a bunch of stolen horses."

"You ain't gonna be caught with nothin'," Parker said. "I guarantee it."

"Not for nothin', Butch," Foreman said, "using Parker's nickname, "but I'll just stay nervous. It's kept me alive for this long."

"Suit yourself."

The dozen ponies went over the rise and disappeared from sight. Parker chased them, rode up to the top and then looked down. The horses were trotting ahead of him, heading for a ranch house and corral.

"There it is," Parker said, as Foreman rode up alongside him.

"It's about time."

They rode down the hill to follow the horses to their destination.

But, as they approached the corral, the horses began to spread out, so Parker and Foreman had to split up to herd the horses back together and drive them forward the rest of the way.

The door to the ranch house opened and a man stepped out, holding a rifle. The gate to the corral was open. Parker and Foreman drove the horses inside, then closed it. That done, they rode to the house, where the man with the rifle waited.

"Are you Parker?" the man asked Foreman.

"No, he is," Foreman said.

"The young one?" the rancher said, in surprise. "I thought—"

"Don't matter what you thought," Parker said. "Are you Dan Winston?"

"That's me."

"We've delivered the horses."

"Come on inside, then," the man said, "and I'll pay you. I'll also give ya somethin' to eat and drink."

"Sounds good," Parker said, dismounting.

Foreman dismounted nervously. He took one last look around before following the other two men into the house.

The outside of the house looked rustic, but the inside was different. More care had been taken with the walls and furnishings. Parker figured it made more sense to spend money on the inside. The outward appearance would keep the house from attracting thieves and outlaws who might think it was worth robbing.

"Whiskey?" the man offered.

"Sure, why not?" Parker said.

Winston put his rifle down, poured three glasses and handed them each one.

"I've got some cold chicken, if you're interested."

"Cold chicken sounds good," Parker said.

"Money sounds better," Foreman said.

"Of course. You're anxious to get paid. The money's in my desk."

The man walked to a small desk in a corner and, with his back to them, opened a drawer. He took something out, and, when he turned, he was holding a gun.

"What the—" Parker said, as he drew his own weapon from his belt.

Foreman started to draw his, but Winston shot him, thinking he should take the older man first. That was his mistake. As he turned to take care of Parker, the young man fired twice, striking the rancher both times. The man staggered, the gun dropping from his hand, and fell onto his face.

Parker rushed to Foreman, who was sitting on the floor, holding his side.

"You see?" the injured man said, "it pays to be nervous."

"How bad are you hit?"

"I don't think it's too bad," Foreman said, "but I'm gonna need some doctorin'."

"There's a town near here, in a box canyon," Parker said. "Columbia. I'll take you there."

"Search the house first," Foreman said. "We drove them horses a long way. We wanna get paid."

"Are you sure?"

"Yeah, yeah," Foreman said, "I'll make it, all right. Just hurry!"

Chapter Four

They took what money they found in the desk, although it wasn't what they had agreed on. Parker didn't want to take the time to search the entire house, even though Foreman wanted him to.

"Come on," he said, helping the older man to his feet, "I gotta get you to a doc."

They staggered outside and Parker asked, "Are you gonna be able to ride?"

"If it's ride or die," Foreman said, "I'll ride. Just help me into the saddle."

Parker helped Foreman climb aboard his horse and get relatively comfortable in the saddle, then mounted his own horse.

"How far is this town?" Foreman asked.

"Not sure," Parker admitted. "I just know it's in the box canyon."

"And it's got a doctor?"

"I ain't sure," Parker said. "But I hope so."

"Jesus," Foreman said.

***

It took longer than Parker figured. Foreman kept passing out, and a couple of times Parker had to keep him from falling off his horse. Each time Foreman growled, "I'm fine!" or "I know how to ride a horse!"

It was dusk when Parker saw the town, and the surrounding mountains dotted with mines.

"It's just up ahead, Earl," he said. "Hang in there."

Foreman didn't answer, and Parker realized the man had passed out in the saddle. He rode alongside rather than leading the horse, so he could reach out and support him, and they rode into Columbia that way.

***

"Does this town have a sawbones?" Parker asked the first person he saw.

"Right down the street, next to the hardware store."

"Much obliged."

He continued on, saw the hardware store, and the door next to it with a shingle hanging outside. It said STEWART ELLIOT, M.D. He reined in his horse in front of the office, climbed down and helped Foreman do the same.

"Come on, Earl," he said, letting the man lean on him, "let's get you took care of."

As Parker slammed the door open, the man inside took one look and didn't hesitate.

"Bring 'im in here," he said, leading the way into another room. "Put him on that table, on his back."

Parker obeyed.

"Now get out," the man said.

"What?"

"I need complete quiet while I treat him," the doctor said. "Go and get yourself a drink and then come back."

"This town got a sheriff?" Parker asked.

"Sort of," the doctor said.

"Whataya mean—"

"Later!" the sawbones said and slammed the door. Parker shrugged and stepped outside. He saw a café across the street and figured, what the hell. At twenty he didn't drink all that much, but he sure was hungry. He crossed the street and went inside.

"Saw you take your friend into the doc's," the waiter said, as Parker sat. "He'll take good care of 'im, whatever's wrong with 'im."

"Good to know," Parker said. "Thanks."

"What'll ya have?" the waiter asked.

"Whataya got?"

"Anythin' you want," the waiter said.

"Fried chicken?"

"Comin' up," the waiter said. "Mashed 'taters?"

"Oh, yeah," Parker said.

"Won't be long."

As the waiter went to the kitchen, Parker stared out the window at the street.

"Not much goin' on here," he said, when the waiter came back with some water.

"Miners'll be down soon for supper, and drinkin'," the man said. "Then everythin' changes."

"You get many strangers in town?" Parker asked.

"Not many, but you're the second—well, with your friend, I guess you're second and third today."

"Is that right?" Parker realized the waiter was a talker, so he didn't really have to ask a lot of questions.

"And he's kinda famous," the waiter said. "His name's Clint Adams."

"The Gunsmith?"

"The same."

"Wonder what he's doin' here?"

"Lookin' for a friend of his," the waiter said. "One of the miners."

"Ah. And you got a lawman?"

"We got us a part-time lawman," the waiter said. "Most of the time he just works in the livery, though. Lemme get that plate for ya."

The waiter went into the kitchen and returned with Parker's fried chicken.

Chapter Five

After he devoured the chicken and everything that came with it, Parker paid his bill and went back across to the doctor's office. The door to the other room was still closed, so he decided to sit and wait. It took only moments for the doctor to appear from the back room.

"Ah, you're here," he said. "Your friend is going to be all right. The bullet hit a lot of fatty tissue, didn't do any major damage. But he lost a lot of blood, so he needs to rest. Get him into a hotel and a bed as soon as you can and leave him there for several days."

"When can I take him?"

"Well, I don't have anybody here, right now," the doctor said. "Let's let him rest here a couple more hours before you try to walk him to the hotel."

"All right," Parker said. "I'll be back for him later. Thanks, Doc. What do I owe you?"

"We can settle up when you come back," the doctor said.

Parker nodded and left the office. He went directly to the Columbia Hotel and got two rooms. When he came back out onto the street, he noticed there were more people there. Apparently, the miners had started to come down from the mountain.

***

Clint was sitting in a chair in front of the hotel when the miners started to fill the street, laughing and slapping each other on the back, heading for a café or saloon. At the same time, a young man came out, stood a few feet away from Clint and also watched.

"They remind me of ranch hands hittin' town after a day's work," the young man said to Clint.

"I was thinking the same thing," Clint said.

The young man turned to face him.

"You don't look like a miner," he said.

"I'm not," Clint said, "and neither are you."

"I just rode in today."

"So did I, earlier this morning," Clint said.

"You got business in town?" the young man asked.

"Why do you ask?"

The young man shrugged.

"I'm stuck here, so I'm just makin' conversation."

"I'm here to see a friend," Clint said. "You?"

"I had to take a friend to the doctor." He stuck out his hand. "My name's Robert Leroy Parker."

Clint shook his hand and said, "Clint Adams."

Parker looked surprised.

"The Gunsmith," Parker said. "You have an interest in a mine?"

"No, just a miner," Clint said. "I don't see him with this group."

The miners went past. Some of them stopped into the café, others went directly to the saloon.

"Well," Parker said, "I've gotta go and get my friend and bring him to the hotel. Maybe I'll see you later."

"Sure," Clint said, "Maybe at the saloon."

"I ain't much of a drinker," Parker said, "but I could stand a beer."

He touched the brim of his hat, stepped into the street and walked off. Clint had never heard of Parker before, so didn't give the young man much thought.

He continued to sit and watch as groups of miners went by, still not spotting Benny Diamond. His friend would have been easy to pick out of a crowd, as he was short and stocky, but filled with energy. If he was walking down the street, he would be noticed.

But before he could spot Benny, Robert Leroy Parker returned, with an older man leaning heavily on him.

"You need some help getting him to a room?" Clint asked.

"That'd be great, thanks," Parker said.

Clint stood and got on the other side of the man. Together they walked him across the lobby and up the stairs to a room, where they deposited him on the bed.

"I've got 'im, now," Parker said. "Thanks for your help, Mr. Adams."

"Just call me Clint. After all, we're going to have a beer together."

"My friends call me Butch," Parker said.

"I'll see you later, Butch."

Clint went back down to his chair in front of the hotel. As darkness fell, he still hadn't seen Benny. He wondered if his friend might have gone by while he was helping Parker with his friend. His only choice was to start checking cafes and saloons to see if he could find him.

***

He went to that second café, the one he was now thinking of as the miner's café. Standing at the door, he saw that the tables were all taken. Miners were eating voraciously, but there was still no sign of Benny.

He went to the first café, where he had eaten. There only a few tables were occupied, but no Benny.

Next, he headed for the saloon.

Chapter Six

Clint entered the Golden Nugget Saloon, which seemed to be catering to most of the miners. He went to the bar, found a space large enough for him to fit into, and waved to the bartender.

"Beer," he said.

The bartender nodded.

Clint looked around. He saw a few men, but none of them looked like miners. The rest were dressed in jeans and work shirts covered with dirt.

The bartender brought the beer and set it down in front of him.

"Do you know Benny Diamond?" he asked the man. "He's one of the miners."

"There are a lot of 'em here," the man said. "I don't know 'em all."

He moved along before Clint could ask him anything else.

Sipping his cold beer, Clint turned and once again examined the interior of the saloon. Benny Diamond wasn't there. A miner standing at the bar with his friends backed into Clint, turned and said, "Sorry, friend."

"No problem, friend," Clint said.

The man, a big miner with broad shoulders, grinned and turned back to the bar.

"Say, maybe you can help me," Clint said.

The big miner turned back.

"With what?"

"I'm looking for a friend of mine," Clint said. "Do you know Benny Diamond?"

"Benny?" the man said "Sure, I know Benny. He's a good man."

"Well, I'm Clint Adams. I'm supposed to be meeting him, but it doesn't look like he came to town tonight."

"Maybe not," the miner said. "We don't all come down, every night."

"What's your name?" Clint asked.

"I'm Jack Hunter," the man said. "Around here they call me Big Jack."

"Well Big Jack, I wonder if you could help me find him?" Clint said.

"If he's in town," Big Jack said, "we'll find 'im. If not, then I'll just take you up to his mine. Howzat?"

"That'd be great," Clint said. "I'd be much obliged."

"But first," Big Jack said, "another beer?"

"On me," Clint said.

"Good man!"

***

After they shared a beer, Big Jack said goodbye to his friends and led Clint out of the saloon.

"Did you check the cafes?" he asked.

"I did."

"Then the only other place is the other saloon," Big Jack said. "Follow me."

Big Jack led him down the street to a smaller saloon called O'GRADY'S. Inside he saw it was about half-filled with some miners, and others who appeared to be locals.

"He's not here, either," Clint said.

"Then he probably stayed up at his mine," Big Jack said.

"Can you take me up there?"

"Sure," Big Jack said, "but not tonight. It gets very dark on that mountain, and, if you don't know the way, you could take a bad step."

"I could step where you step," Clint told him.

"Still," Big Jack said, "it's not safe. Let's have another beer while we're here."

"Sure," Clint said. "Why not?"

They went to the bar and got a beer each, stood there and drank together.

"You know," Big Jack said, "there's one other thing we can try."

"What's that?"

"Not what, actually," Big Jack said, "but who."

"Okay, who?" Clint asked.

"Petey Driscoll," Big Jack said. "He has the claim nearest to Benny's operation. We could find him, ask him if he's seen 'im."

"Is this Petey Driscoll a friend of Benny's?" Clint asked him.

"Friend?" Big Jack smiled broadly. "No, he's just a neighbor."

"Where would he be?"

"Petey feeds his face before he starts drinkin'," Big Jack said. "He's probably in one of the cafes."

Clint finished his beer and set the empty glass down on the bar.

"Let's go and check."

Big Jack laughed, drained his beer, slammed the glass down and led the way from the saloon.

Driscoll wasn't in the miner's café, so they walked to the other end of town to check the first one.

Chapter Seven

The waiter recognized Clint from earlier.

"Back again?"

"But not to eat," Clint said, "not this time, anyway. I'm just looking for somebody."

"And I don't see 'im here," Big Jack said. "Let's try the saloon, again."

"Come back soon," the waiter called.

Clint and Big Jack walked to the Golden Nugget.

"See him?" Clint asked.

"Benny or Driscoll?" Big Jack said.

"Either one."

"No," Jack said, "but I see a friend of Driscoll's. Come on."

When they reached Driscoll's friend, it turned out to be a man involved in an arm wrestling contest. Of the two men, one was very large with bulging arms, the other smaller, who was obviously using leverage to overcome brute strength.

Clint leaned over and asked Big Jack, "Which one is Driscoll's friend?"

"The smaller one," Jack said. "His name's Freddy Moran."

As they watched, Moran and the big man went back and forth while their friends gathered around and urged them on. Finally, the smaller Moran pinned the larger man, who simply laughed about it, shaking his head, and bought the victor a beer.

"Freddy," Big Jack called, as the man stood up. He was barely five-foot-four.

"Hey, Jack," Moran said. "What kin I do for ya?"

"This is a friend of Benny Diamond's," Jack said. "He's lookin' for 'im. Have you seen 'im?"

Moran frowned.

"Not today, I ain't. Fact is, I don't think I've seen Benny in a few days, but I been real busy with my own work."

"Well, thanks, anyway," Big Jack said.

He and Clint moved away and found an empty table to sit at. As they did, a girl Clint hadn't seen before came over and asked if they wanted anything.

"Two beers," Clint said.

"Comin' up."

For a saloon girl, she was pretty enough, but plainly dressed in a cotton skirt and blouse.

"Yeah," Big Jack said, as if reading Clint's mind, "in mining camps the girls are really just here to serve drinks, so they don't bother with fancy gowns to show themselves off."

"What do the miners do for female companionship?" Clint asked.

"Some of them have wives and women in their camps," Jack said. "For others, there are a couple of whores in a house at the end of town."

"You think Benny might be there?" Clint asked.

"Hah," Jack laughed, "Benny don't bother with whores. He's . . . what? Sixty-five? All he's interested in is gold."

The girl came back with their beers, then flounced off to serve others.

"Jack," Clint said, "I want to go up the mountain with you."

"In the dark?" Jack reminded him.

"Most of you go back up to your mines after the saloon and cafes close, don't you?"

"Well, yeah," Jack said. "That's where we live, and we know the way blindfolded."

"Well, I'll just follow close behind you," Clint said. "I want to see Benny's mine."

"Okay," Jack said, "have it your way—but I ain't goin' back up for a while."

"I'll be right here, waiting," Clint said. "Just come and get me."

"You got it," Jack said, standing. "Thanks for the beer.

The big man went off to drink and talk with some of his fellow miners.

***

Robert Leroy Parker decided he needed to do something other than sit in his hotel room. He left the hotel, confident that Foreman was asleep in his room, recovering.

On the street Parker could see that the Golden Nugget was the liveliest place, so he walked over and entered. It was filled with miners, still covered with the grime of their day's work. But at one table he saw Clint Adams seated alone, so he walked over.

"Mind if I join you?" he asked.

"Hey, no," Clint said, "don't mind at all. I said I'd buy you a beer. Have a seat."

As Parker sat, Clint beckoned the girl over. She was young and gave Parker a wide smile.

"Can I get you somethin'?" she asked him.

"Bring my friend a beer," Clint said, "and another for me."

"Comin' up." She smiled at Parker again, then headed for the bar.

Chapter Eight

"How's your friend doing?" Clint asked.

"He's asleep," Parker said. "Thanks again for helpin' me get 'im up the stairs."

"No problem."

The girl came back and set their drinks down.

"I'm Jackie," she said to Parker. "Let me know if you want anythin' else."

"We will," Clint said. As she walked away, he said to Parker, "She likes you."

"She does?" Parker asked. "How can you tell?"

"You can't tell?"

"I ain't had much luck with girls," the young man said.

"Well," Clint said, "she was smiling at you, and ignoring me."

"Aw, c'mon," Parker said.

"Take my word for it, Butch," Clint said. "She likes you."

"Okay," Parker said.

"By the way," Clint said, "where's the name Butch come from?"

"I use'ta work in a butcher shop," Parker said.

"Ah," Clint said, "that makes sense. A lot of nicknames don't."

"Like your nickname?" Parker asked.

"I'm afraid that's not a nickname," Clint said. "It's a label, and after all these years, it's permanent. Besides, I really am a gunsmith."

"But it's also a reputation," Parker said, "and it's an amazin' one. It's like . . . 'Wild Bill' Hickok."

"I'd never compare myself to Jim Hickok," Clint said.

"Did you know 'im?" Parker asked.

"He was my best friend," Clint said. "That is, until a coward's bullet put an end to his life."

"You were best friends with Wild Bill?" Parker said, in awe. "That's amazin'."

"Don't be so impressed by reputations, Butch."

"Why not?" Parker said. "I'm gonna have one of my own, some day."

"Just think twice about the kind of rep you want," Clint told him. "That's the only advice I'm going to give you."

When they finished their beers, Clint asked the young man if he wanted another.

"Naw," Parker replied, "like I said, I ain't much of a drinker."

"Well then maybe you should just talk to Jackie before you leave."

Parker suddenly appeared very shy.

"I—I can't," he said. "I gotta get back and check on my friend." He stood up, said, "Thanks for the beer," and hurried out.

Jackie came over moments later and asked Clint, "Where's your friend?"

"He had to go back to the hotel," Clint said.

"Is he comin' back?"

"I don't know."

"He sure is pretty," she said, and walked away.

At that point, Clint saw a second woman appear and start to work the floor. She was older than Jackie, tall, with a full, mature body beneath her simple skirt and blouse. Her hair was long and red, and as she passed by close enough, he saw her green eyes and freckles. She was the picture of a perfect redhead.

He decided to have another beer . . .

***

The woman's name was Dixie, and when she brought Clint his beer, he asked her to sit with him.

"Well," she said, "only for a while. I got lots of thirsty miners, here." She sat across from him. "You're a stranger. I ain't seen you in here before."

"I just rode in today," Clint said.

"You ain't lookin' for work in a mine, I can tell that by lookin' at ya," she said.

"No," he said, "but I am looking for a miner, a friend of mine named Benny Diamond."

Her eyebrows went up.

"I know Benny. He comes in here a lot." She looked around. "Fact is, I'm surprised he ain't here tonight."

"Is that unusual?" Clint asked.

"Pretty much, since he's in here most nights," she told him.

That wasn't exactly what he had heard from others who had given him the impression that Benny didn't come down from his mine every night.

"I got work to do, since I just came on," she said. "But we can talk later, if you like. I don't get to talk to anybody but miners, usually. It'll be a nice change."

"I'd be happy to oblige, Dixie."

She smiled, stood and said, "See ya later, then."

"Maybe tomorrow," he said. "I've got to go up to Benny's mine tonight."

"In the dark?" she asked. "I'd be real careful if I was you."

"I'm going to have a guide."

"Still," she said, "it's pretty dangerous up there."

"I'll watch my step," he promised.

Chapter Nine

Clint was sitting alone, watching Dixie work the floor, when Big Jack came over, weaving a bit from the beers he'd been drinking.

"I'm ready to go," he said, "if ya still wanna come with me."

"I do."

"Good," the big man said, "because I'm probably gonna need you to keep me from fallin' off the mountain."

"I'll do my best," Clint promised.

They left the saloon and started walking down the street. Big Jack was already weaving and in need of Clint's guidance to walk straight. When they reached the end of the street, they started on a path that led upward.

"This takes us up to the mines," Big Jack said. "It's wide down here, but it gets more narrow further up. Just walk where I walk."

"Got it."

"And if I start to fall," Jack added, "catch me. Ready?"

"I'm ready," Clint said.

They started up.

"How far is Benny's claim?"

"Not as far as mine," Jack said. "It's one of the mines that's lower on the mountain."

"That's good."

"I'll show you where it is," Big Jack said, "but you still gotta walk me to my mine."

"Then I'll have to come back down in the dark, alone," Clint said.

"You should remember the way," Jack said. "Or I can put you up for the night, and you can start back down in the mornin'."

"I have a third suggestion," Clint said. "You and I can check Benny's mine. Once I know he's there, I'll walk you up to yours."

"Agreed."

***

As promised, the path began to get narrowed the higher they went. Once or twice Jack's big foot slipped, and Clint had to steady him.

"Easy, big fella," Clint said, the second time.

"We're almost to Benny's mine," Jack said.

"There are none lower than his?" Clint asked.

"Some played out mines, but nothin' that's bein' worked right now."

They passed some of those dead mines, the entrances boarded up to send the message that they were, indeed, played out.

"We're comin' to Benny's," Jack said, and pointed to a board with THE DIAMOND MINE written on it.

"Clever," Clint said.

They came to a clearing in front of an entrance. There was a cold campfire, and a handmade wooden chair. Off to one side was a bedroll.

"This is how Benny lives?" he asked.

"It's how we all live," Jack said. "If the weather turns, we sleep inside the mine. If it gets really cold, then we have to go to town. Some of the larger mines have more room outside, and they've actually built some shacks."

Clint walked to the remnants of the fire and placed his hand on the ashes.

"Still warm." He stood and looked around, then called out, "Benny! Benny Diamond?"

His voice echoed, but there was no answer.

"That's odd," Jack said. "If he ain't here and he ain't in town . . ."

"We could look inside," Clint said, "unless you just want to keep going to your own camp?"

"Let's have a look," Big Jack said.

They walked to the mouth of the mine, picked up an oil lamp that was on the ground and lit it.

"You're still better off followin' me," Jack said.

"Lead on," Clint said.

They entered the mine.

***

Parker stopped at Foreman's room to check on his friend. He found him sleeping peacefully. Satisfied, he went to his own room to get some rest. Meeting the Gunsmith had been very unexpected. He was impressed by the man and would have liked to spend more time with him. But he had killed a man while delivering stolen horses to him. He didn't know how Clint Adams would react to that, so he had to try to make sure he never found out.

He had to stay in Columbia until Earl Foreman recovered, and then they could both move on. They could do that as long as nobody discovered the dead body. He was sorry now that he couldn't have taken the time to bury Dan Winston's body. Somebody was sure to find him eventually, but the only question was, when?

Chapter Ten

Clint followed closely behind Big Jack, who was holding the lantern up high.

"Benny!" Jack called out. "Benny, you in here?"

No answer.

They reached a point where an empty wheelbarrow was lying on its side. There was also a variety of hand tools strewn about, hammers and pickaxes of varying sizes.

"This don't look good," Jack said.

"Why not? Looks like somebody's been working, here," Clint said.

"Benny's the type to clean up at the end of the day," Jack said. "He'd never leave his tools lying around like this."

"So you're saying something happened to him," Clint said. "This is all the indication of a struggle?"

"Could be."

"Has anyone been after Benny's claim?" Clint asked. "Does he have any enemies on this mountain?"

"Benny's claim ain't big enough for anybody to wanna steal," Jack said.

"So then this mess has no explanation."

"It ain't that it don't have one," Jack said. "I just can't think what it might be."

"What if Benny had a big strike and didn't keep quiet about it?"

"I woulda heard somethin'," Big Jack said. "Can't be that."

They continued to search the interior of the mine, but there was no sign of Benny Diamond. They turned around and went back outside, where it was pitch black.

At that moment, a couple of other miners appeared, walking up the path to their own claims.

"Either of you fellas seen Benny Diamond lately?" Big Jack asked.

They both just shrugged and shook their heads as they went by.

"There ain't much more we can do til mornin'," Big Jack said. "You can try to get back down by yourself in the dark, or come with me, and I'll put you up for the night in my camp."

"Is your camp like this?"

"Bigger," Jack said, "with a shack."

Clint shivered against the cold of the night and said, "I'll come with you."

"Good," Jack said. "I have a warm fire, and some good whiskey. In the mornin' I'll help you find Benny."

"That works for me," Clint said.

He followed Big Jack the rest of the way to his camp. There was already a fire going, with three men seated at it.

“This is my crew,” Big Jack said, offering no names. “This is Clint Adams. He’s my guest tonight.”

“Adams, the Gunsmith?” one of them asked.

“That’s right,” Jack said.

The three miners had such smudged faces that Clint couldn’t tell their ages.

“Coffee?” one of them asked.

“Yes, please,” Clint said.

“Sit,” the man said, and held a cup out to him.

Clint accepted the cup and sat by the fire. Jack sat across from him.

“Bulldog is my cook,” Jack said. “That is, when I don’t go down the mountain to eat.”

Clint sipped the coffee, found it strong and black, the way he liked it.

“Good coffee,” he said.

“Wait until you taste his breakfast,” Jack said. “Clint, you can sleep in the shack tonight. But first, let’s sweeten that coffee.”

Jack stood, went to the shack, and came back with a bottle of whiskey.

“The rest of you can turn in,” Jack said.

The three men nodded, stood up and walked to their bed rolls. Jack leaned forward and poured a generous dollop of whiskey into Clint's coffee.

"Do they usually sleep in the shack?" Clint asked.

"No, they sleep outside," Jack said. "I usually sleep in the shack, but tonight it's yours."

"I appreciate that."

He drank the coffee, and the whiskey burned its way down, warming him.

"Do you want somethin' to eat before you turn in?" Jack asked.

"No, I'm fine," Clint said. "I haven't seen Benny in years. He wouldn't leave his mine, would he?"

"None of us would," Big Jack said. "We've worked too hard to get them up and runnin'."

"So he's got to be around here someplace," Clint said. "What about the two prostitutes?"

"It's possible, I guess," Jack said. "I just know that Benny hasn't shown interest in women in a long time. I think it'd be odd for him to start now."

"There's no harm in checking," Clint said.

"No, there ain't. I'll take you to see them in the mornin'."

"I don't want to interfere with your business," Clint said.

"That's okay," Jack said. "My crew will keep at it. To tell the truth, now I'm a little worried about Benny, too."

Jack gave Clint a blanket he could use and sent him off to sleep in the shack.

Chapter Eleven

Clint woke the next morning and could smell the bacon from outside. Stomach growling, he stood up, strapped on his gun, and walked to the door. When he opened it, he saw the cook, Bulldog, hunched over the fire. Off to the side Big Jack and the other two crew members were getting to their feet and stretching. Apparently, they had also been awakened by the smell.

Clint left the shack and walked to the fire. Bulldog saw him and poured him a cup of coffee.

"There ya go," the man said. "Breakfast is almost ready."

"Smells great," Clint said.

"How'd you sleep?" Big Jack asked, joining him by the fire.

"I slept like a log," Clint said. "I appreciate the hospitality."

"Hey, you're a friend of Benny's," Jack said. "Any friend of a miner is a friend of all miners."

The other two came over and soon they were all drinking coffee, waiting for Bulldog to hand them a plate. When he did, Clint was surprised to find Johnny cakes and bacon on his plate.

"These are good," he said, surprised, when he tasted them.

"I told you, didn't I?" Big Jack said. "Bulldog's a good cook."

"Why do you even go down to town to eat, then?" Clint asked.

"Because I go to the saloon after for some relaxation," Jack said. "And if I stayed up here all the time and ate his cookin', I'd get fat."

"I can believe that," Clint said.

"Some maple syrup for your Johnny cakes, Mr. Adams?" Bulldog asked.

"Pour it on, Bulldog," Clint said, holding out his plate.

***

Before Clint and Big Jack started back down the mountain, Jack gave his crew their orders for the day.

"You trust them to do their work while you're gone?" Clint asked.

"They're all good boys," Jack said. "Besides, they know if they steal from me, I'll bust their heads."

They headed to town to look for Benny Diamond.

***

Parker woke early and went to Foreman's room to check on him. He was awake, sitting up in bed.

"How you feelin', Earl?" he asked.

"Better," Foreman said. "And hungry. I think I'll go downstairs for some breakfast."

"Doc says you gotta rest," Parker said. "I'll bring somethin' up for ya."

"You don't gotta do that, Butch," Foreman said.

"Just sit tight," Parker said. "I'll be right back. Flapjacks okay?"

"That'll do fine," Foreman said, "just fine. And maybe some bacon."

"Comin' up," Parker said.

***

Parker brought Foreman his breakfast but didn't wait for him to eat it. He put the tray on his bed, made sure the man could feed himself, then turned to leave, saying he would check in later.

"Hold on a minute. What about the law?" Foreman asked. "Has anybody—do you know if the body's been found?"

"I haven't heard anythin'," Parker said. "But I do know there's just a part-time sheriff here. Mostly he runs the livery stable."

"Well, that's good," Foreman said. "I don't like the idea of bein' a sittin' duck, up here, for some lawman."

"Don't worry," Parker said. "If I hear anythin', we'll get out of this town."

"What goes on here, anyway?"

"It's pretty quiet until the miners come down at night, to eat and drink. Then it can get pretty rowdy. Oh, and there's somebody else in town who don't belong here—Clint Adams."

"The Gunsmith?" Foreman asked, while he ate. "What's he doin' here?"

"Visitin' some miner friend of his. At least, that's what he says."

"You and him talked?"

"He's stayin' in this hotel," Parker said. "We met out front. Don't worry about him, Earl. He's just passin' through, like us."

"Well," Foreman said, "thanks for the breakfast. I'll see ya later."

"I'll check on ya at lunch time," Parker said.

"Thanks, Butch."

Parker left the hotel room and went in search of his own breakfast.

Chapter Twelve

When they got back to town, Big Jack took Clint to the other end, to a small house he said the two whores used.

"Just two?" Clint asked. "It's not a full cathouse?"

"Naw," Big Jake said, "they don't have to work for anybody. They work for themselves."

It was a one-story, wood frame house that needed some paint and carpentry, but apparently the two women were worried about what went on inside, not outside.

They went to the front door and Jack knocked. They waited and eventually the door was opened by a tall girl with long blonde hair and a pretty face. She looked to be in her thirties and was wearing a dress with the fabric so thin Clint could see the outline of her body. She had small breasts, but very large nipples. She had definite appeal.

"Big Jack," she said, "what the hell are you doin' here so early? Why ain't you workin'?"

"This is a friend of mine, Brenda," Jack said, "and he's lookin' for a friend of his, Benny Diamond."

"Benny," she said frowning, then brightened. "Ain't he an old fella? White hair, kinda bow-legged?"

"That's him," Clint said. "Have you seen him?"

"In town, sure," she said, "but he don't come around here."

"Seen him lately?" Clint asked.

She looked at Clint and said, "Can't say I have, handsome, but you wanna come in and take a look?" She swung the door open wide and smiled.

"No," Clint said, "that's all right. I'll take your word for it."

"Whatsamatta, honey?" she asked. "Don't you like girls?"

"I love girls," Clint said, "I just don't pay for them."

"Oh," she said, "you must be somethin' special, then."

"Look, my friend seems to be missing," Clint said. "If you happen to see him, would you leave me a message at the Columbia hotel? My name's Clint Adams."

"Clint—" she started, then stopped. "Okay, Mr. Adams, you got a deal. If I see 'im, I'll let ya know."

"And tell Molly, too," Big Jack said.

"I will," she said. "We'll both be on the lookout for 'im."

"I appreciate that," Clint said. "Thanks."

He turned and went back along the walkway to the street. Behind him he thought he heard some whispering, and the girl said "Gunsmith," loud enough for him to hear. Then he heard Jack say, "Just keep yer eyes open," and that was that.

***

Parker was in the café the miners didn't use much, having a breakfast that he was finding very satisfying. When he looked out the window, he saw Clint Adams walk by with a big miner. He assumed Adams was still looking for his friend. He saw no point in calling out to the man and kept eating.

***

Clint and Big Jack headed down the street toward Clint's hotel. Where else was there to go? They had already eaten breakfast, and the saloon wasn't open yet.

"We could try the mercantile," Jack said, "and see when he was in for supplies."

"Sounds good," Clint said. "Lead on."

Big Jack took Clint to the mercantile. It was a small, but cluttered store that seemed to have everything a miner could need. There were several men taking items from shelves, and a couple at the counter paying for their purchase. Clint and Jack waited until the clerk was done and then stepped up.

"Hey, Big Jack," the sixtyish clerk said, "whataya need today?"

"Nothin' really, Ivan," Jack said. "This is Clint Adams. He's a friend of Benny Diamond and came to town yesterday lookin' for him."

"Ain't he up at his mine?"

"No," Jack said, "and it looks like maybe he ain't been there for a few days. Have you seen him?"

"Can't say I have," Ivan answered.

"Do you know when you did see him last?" Clint asked.

"Hmm, let's see," the man said, rubbing his jaw, "I think he was in last week buyin' some grub—beans, bacon, canned peaches. Yeah, I think that was the last time."

"Would you say you usually see him in here every week?" Clint asked.

"Pretty much," Ivan said. "Most of the miners need somethin' or other every week, wouldn't you say, Jack?"

"I would," Jack said. "Grub, tools, soap—"

"Ain't too many of you miners buyin' soap," Ivan said.

"Hey," Big Jack replied, "some of us use soap, once in a while."

"Whiskey's more like it," Ivan said.

"Does Benny buy a lot of whiskey?" Clint asked. He didn't recall the old miner being a heavy drinker.

"Naw, he'd buy a bottle once in a while, but Benny ain't never been a drinker," Ivan said, as if reading Clint's mind.

"I'm at the Columbia Hotel," Clint said. "If you see him would you let me know?"

"Sure thing, Mr. Adams," the clerk said.

Clint and Jack left the store, stopped just outside.

"I gotta get back to work, Clint," Jack said. "How about we meet up later at the saloon for a beer?"

"Sounds good, Jack. Thanks for your help."

As Big Jack walked away, heading toward his mine, the talk of soap led Clint to think about a bath.

Chapter Thirteen

By the time he finished with his bath, the saloons were open, so Clint went into the Golden Nugget for a beer. The bartender served it to him without comment. It was the same man he had asked the day before if he knew Benny Diamond. He had the feeling the man had lied to him. He hadn't pushed it at first, but now it seemed that Benny was missing.

"I asked you about Benny Diamond yesterday," Clint said to the man.

"Huh, didja?" the bartender asked. "I don't remember."

"I think you do," Clint said, "and I think yesterday you lied to me."

The bartender was beefy and brusque.

"Who d'ya think you are, callin' me a liar?" he demanded.

"The name's Clint Adams. Benny's a friend of mine, and it looks like he's missing. So, if you're lying to me, then maybe you've got something to do with that."

The bartender thought a moment, then said, "So you're the Gunsmith?"

"That's right."

"You shoulda told me that yesterday," the bartender said. "Yeah, I know Benny, but I ain't seen him in a while."

"How long is a while?" Clint asked.

"A few days, I guess."

"And when you saw him, it was in here?"

"Well, sure," the barman said, "where else?"

"Who was he with?"

"What?"

"If he was in here, was he drinking with somebody?" Clint asked.

"I guess . . ."

"You guess?" Clint asked. "You don't know?"

"Benny usually kept to himself," the bartender said. "He'd stand at the bar, have one beer, and then leave. Oh, wait . . ."

"What?"

"I just thought of somethin'," the barman said. "I think Benny was talking to Dixie."

Clint looked around.

"Is she here?"

"She ain't come down yet from her room," the bartender said.

"Can I go up?"

"She's probably asleep," the bartender said. "She wouldn't like it if you woke 'er."

"Might be worth it if she can help me," Clint said. "I'll chance it."

The bartender shrugged.

"That's up to you," he said. "Room two."

"Thanks."

Clint drank his beer, then walked across the floor to the stairs and went up. He found room two and knocked. Dixie opened the door right away, smiled when she saw him. She was wearing a robe, belted at the waist, with a good portion of cleavage revealed.

"Well, well," she said, "I didn't expect to see you up here."

"The bartender told me I might be waking you up," Clint said.

"Oh, I've been awake for a while," she said. "It takes me some time to put on my face, you know. I ain't as young as I used to be."

"You look plenty good, and you know it."

"Just for that," she said, "I'll invite you in."

She backed away to allow him to enter.

"Close the door," she said.

"You sure?" he asked.

"Positive."

He closed it.

"I'm not dressed," she said.

"I noticed."

"Do you mind if I keep working on my face?"

"Not at all."

She sat at her dressing table and eyed him in the mirror.

"What can I do for you?"

"The bartender—I don't know his name."

"Lou."

"Yeah, well, Lou told me he saw you talking to Benny Diamond a few nights ago."

"I know Benny," she said. "He comes in here every once in a while. He's a nice old guy."

"Do you remember what you were talking about?"

She turned so she could look straight at him.

"Is there a problem?"

"I came to town to see Benny," he said. "Only he seems to have disappeared."

"And you checked his mine?"

"I checked everywhere he might be," Clint said, "and some places I knew he wouldn't be."

"Oh, the girls," she said.

"Yes."

"No, he wouldn't be there," she agreed. "All right, wait a minute—a few nights ago, you said?"

"That's right."

"Let me think."

He eyed her breasts and said, "Take your time."

Chapter Fourteen

Parker didn't know what to do.

With Foreman once again asleep, the young man didn't have anybody to talk to. And he wasn't looking to make any new friends. He just wanted Foreman to recover enough for them to leave. According to the doc, that would take days. There was only one person he thought he could have a conversation with, and that was the other stranger in town—Clint Adams. He also wouldn't mind spending some time with a man who was a legend.

He left his hotel and headed for the Golden Nugget, hoping to find Clint there.

When he entered and saw how empty the place was, he figured he was out of luck. Maybe he should have tried Adams' room at the hotel before he left there.

He went to the bar.

"Whataya want?" the barkeep asked.

"I'll take a beer."

The bartender nodded, set him up with a cold beer. He wasn't one of those talkative bartenders and busied himself wiping the bar down.

"I don't suppose you've seen Clint Adams today, have ya?" Parker asked.

"Who's askin'?"

"A friend of his," Parker said.

"He was in here lookin' for a friend of his," the bartender said, "but you ain't him."

"Look," Parker said, "we both got to town yesterday, and I just wanted to talk to him, that's all."

"He's upstairs, visitin' one of the girls," the bartender said. "You can wait."

"Thanks," Parker said, "I will."

He took his beer to a table and sat. While he was sitting there, he saw the girl, Jackie, coming down the stairs. She didn't look like she was dressed for work. She had on a simple purple dress and flat shoes. After speaking briefly to the bartender, she looked over at him. She smiled and walked over. He hurriedly got to his feet.

"Well, hello," she said.

"H-hello."

"I ain't workin' yet, but do you mind if I sit?"

"No, I don't mind."

"Thank you."

As she sat, he remained standing.

"You can sit down, now," she said.

"Oh, sure." He sat down, stared across the table at her and swallowed.

"Lou tells me you're waitin' for your friend to come down," she said.

"That's right."

"Well," she said, "from the sounds I heard comin' from Dixie's room, I think he might be a while."

"The sounds?"

"You know," she said, "the sounds a man and a woman make—you've made those sounds, haven't you?"

"Huh? Oh, sure, I . . . guess."

"Well," she said, "if you've got the time, you and me could go up to my room and make the same sounds."

"Um, I ain't got much money."

"I'm not a whore, honey," she said.

"Oh, geez," he said, "I'm sorry, I didn't mean—"

"I'm just tryin' to be friendly," she said, reaching across the table and touching his hand. "You're about the prettiest thing I seen come through this town in a long time."

"Um . . ." Parker felt himself blush, and his hand burned where she was touching it.

"Come on," she said, closing her hand over his, "I won't hurt you."

He stood up and she tugged him across the floor to the stairway. They went up, and she stopped in front of the door to room two.

She pressed her ear to the door and waved at him to do the same. When he did, he heard grunts and groans of two voices, and the sound of bedsprings.

"See what I mean?" she whispered.

"I do."

She held her forefinger to her lips, took his hand and led him further along the hall. When they reached room four, she said, "This is mine."

She opened the door and went inside. He remained out in the hall.

"It's okay," she told him, "you can come in."

Hurriedly, he stepped inside the room. She was seated on the edge of her bed, one leg crossed over the other, so that he could see most of the shapely limb. Her shoes were on the floor. He couldn't take his eyes off her toes.

"You can close the door."

He closed it, then turned back and looked at her toes, again.

"Come and sit next to me," she invited, "and we'll talk . . . for a while."

Chapter Fifteen

"You know," Dixie said, "Benny and me, we never have any real deep discussions. Sometimes I just listen to him complain."

"Complain about what?" Clint asked.

"Oh, things," she said. "Other miners, the price of food, warm beer . . . he usually looks for somethin' to complain about."

"Why to you?"

"I dunno," she said, shrugging. "I guess because I listen."

The shrug caused her robe to open, revealing more of what was underneath, which was a lot of smooth, pale skin. She didn't seem to notice—or did and didn't care.

"So that night . . ." Clint prompted.

"He was sayin' that some of the other miners were gettin' impatient."

"About what?"

"Their claims weren't payin' off," she said.

"He didn't complain about his own?"

"Oh, no," she said, "he seemed happy about that. In fact . . . now I remember . . . he was sayin' he thought some of them might be gettin' to the point where they'd try to steal somebody's claim."

Clint found that interesting. The inside of Benny's mine did look as if a struggle might have taken place.

"It sounds like I should start talking to some of the other miners," he said. "I mean, there's no place else to look."

She looked up at him and said, "I can think of a place."

"Where?"

She stood up, dropped her robe to the floor, and said, "Search me."

***

Parker was nervous, and Jackie could see that. She thought it was sweet. She didn't like bringing men up to her room because the men in Columbia were brutes. Let them go to the end of the street to the two whores who got paid for their services. But this boy . . . he was different.

He sat next to her on the bed, nervously.

"Do you mind when I tell you that you're pretty?" she asked.

"I guess not," he said. "You're real pretty, too."

"Oh," she said, "you noticed."

"Well, yeah," he said, "I noticed."

She stood up, then, turned to face him.

"Lemme know what you notice now," she said, and began undressing.

Parker swallowed and watched as she tossed her clothing aside. When she was naked, his mouth went dry.

"So, whataya see?" she asked, putting her hands on her slender hips. She was a small girl, with tiny breasts topped by dark nipples, but Parker hadn't seen that many naked girls. To him, she looked like a goddess. It was almost as if her pale skin was glowing.

"I—I—" he said.

"Never mind," she said, walking up to him and placing her hands on his shoulders, "just kiss me . . ."

***

Dixie had large, heavy breasts and wide hips. She was a big, solid girl, the kind Clint always thought was built for bed.

"What are you thinkin'?" she asked him.

He walked over to her, got close enough to feel the heat emanating from her body.

"I'm thinking I shouldn't be thinking," he said, grabbing her and kissing her. She leaned into the kiss, and opened her mouth, pressing her breasts against his chest.

"That's more like it," she said, breaking the kiss. "Let's get you out of these clothes, handsome. You can use some relaxation."

Together they got him naked, and he hung his gun-belt on the bedpost.

"I guess you've gotta keep that close, huh?" she asked. "With your reputation?"

"Close as I can."

"Well," she said, wrapping her arms around his neck, "you won't be needin' it tonight."

She pulled him down onto the bed with her.

***

When Parker was inside Jackie, he thought he was going to explode.

"Easy, baby," Jackie told him, "slow down."

They were naked on the bed, and his penis was buried inside her. He had never felt anything so hot before. He tried to slow down.

"There you go, that's it," she said, stroking his back, "easy does it. There's no hurry, at all."

Chapter Sixteen

With Dixie on her back in bed, Clint began to explore her body with his hands and mouth.

"Oh God," she said, when his face was pressed to her crotch. She reached down and cupped the back of his head. "I ain't had it this good in a loooooong time."

Instead of pausing to comment, Clint just kept licking and sucking on her until her body began to tremble and she stifled a scream. At that point, she reached for him to draw him up on top of her, so she could take him inside.

"Oh Lord," she gasped, as his cock glided into her. "Oh, yessssss . . ."

He began moving in-and-out of her, slowly at first, and then faster until the sound of their flesh slapping together filled the air.

"Oh Jesus," she said, to him, "I'm gonna scream, but don't worry, they won't hear us downstairs. Just . . . oooh . . . keep doin' what you're doin'!"

Since that was no hardship, he slid his hands beneath her to cup her buttocks, and kept doing what he was doing . . .

***

When Parker finally exploded inside of Jackie, he let out a loud roar, and then immediately shut his mouth.

"Oh, don't worry, honey," she said. "They can't hear us downstairs."

"What about down the hall?" he asked.

"Don't worry about them, either," she said. "Remember, they're makin' their own noise."

He rolled off of her and onto his back.

"That was . . . I don't know what that was," he said. "I ain't smart enough to come up with the words."

"Amazin'?" she asked.

"Well . . . yeah!"

She propped herself up on her elbow next to him and made circles on his chest with her finger.

"Honey," she said, "ain't you been with a girl before?"

"Well, sure," he said, and then added, "like, a whore . . . but never a nice girl, like you."

"So you think I'm a nice girl?"

"You're real nice," he said.

"You're sweet," she said, leaning over to kiss him. Then she slid her hand down between his legs and grabbed him. "Ooh, and you're ready to go again, ain't ya?"

"I sure am," he said, rolling on top of her.

***

Dixie wrestled Clint onto his back so she could ride him instead of the other way around.

"Now you can lie back while I do all the work," she told him.

But as she bounced up and down on him, her breasts bobbed about in front of him, and he couldn't ignore them. He reached out and grabbed them, holding them so he could take the nipples into his mouth. She kept her hips busy, and once again the sound of flesh-on-flesh filled the room, accompanied by her grunt each time she came down on him.

"Oh yeah," she said, "this is it . . . just like this . . . can you keep goin'?"

Clint said through clenched teeth, "I'll keep going as long as you do."

She laughed, came down on him yet again, and said, "We'll see."

***

Jackie watched as Parker got dressed.

"What are you gonna do now, honey?" she asked.

"I think I'd like a beer," Parker said.

"And you should probably eat somethin'," she said. "I think I pretty much drained you."

He walked to the bed and looked down at her.

"Can we do this again?" he asked.

"I don't see why not," she said, "if you really want to."

"Oh, I do," Parker assured her.

"Well, okay, then," she said, smiling up at him.

"When?"

"Well, I don't know that, honey," she said. "But I've got work to do today, so you better get goin'."

"All right," he said, "I'll see you later?"

"Yeah," she said, "later."

He went to the door and stepped out of the room into the hallway. As he started down the hall, the door to room two opened and Clint Adams stepped out. The two men looked at each other.

"Why do I get the feeling we both had the same experience up here?" Clint asked.

"Well," Parker said, "I did hear some noise—"

"I could use a beer," Clint said, cutting him off, "how about you?"

Chapter Seventeen

After Clint dressed and left Dixie sprawled on the bed, he was surprised to step into the hall and find Parker there. Then he remembered how Jackie liked the young man.

"Why do I get the feeling we both had the same experience up here?" he asked.

"Well," Parker said, "I did hear some noise—"

"I could use a beer," Clint said, "how about you?"

"Definitely."

They went downstairs, got two beers from the bar, and went to a table. There were some other patrons in the saloon, but the miners hadn't started to file in, yet.

When they were settled Clint said, "You know, I never asked you how your friend got shot, Butch."

"It was a business transaction gone wrong," Parker said.

"So it turned into a shoot-out?"

Parker stared at Clint, then said, "I'm gonna tell you the truth because you ain't a lawman."

"Go ahead."

"We delivered some horses and were supposed to get paid," Parker said, "but instead, the buyer tried to kill us.

Earl got shot, I drew and killed the buyer. Then I brought Earl here, for a doctor to patch him up. When he's ready, we'll have to move on, because somebody's gonna find the buyer's body."

"You could explain what happened." Clint said. "The law takes self-defense into account."

Parker looked away.

"Ah," Clint said, "the horses weren't yours."

"Well," Parker said, "they weren't, and then they were."

"I got it," Clint said. "You're a young man, Butch. You sure you want to work the wrong side of the law?"

"It was just some easy money, Clint," Parker said. "I didn't even steal the horses, I was just delivering them."

"Well," Clint said, "I'm sure not one to tell you how to live your life."

"How about you?" Parker asked. "Still lookin' for your friend?"

"I am," Clint said. "It looks like I might have to start questioning the miners."

"Don't they kinda stick together?"

"Pretty much," Clint said. "I found one who was willing to help me, but he had to go back to work. I'm supposed to meet him here for a beer, later."

"Why don't I stick with ya," Parker said, "just in case there's trouble."

"Why would you want to buy into my problem?" Clint asked.

Parker shrugged.

"I got nothin' better to do," he said. "Besides, yer a legend. I wouldn't mind seein' you in action."

Clint studied the young man, then said, "You know what, Butch? I'm going to take you up on that offer."

"That's great!"

They raised their beer mugs to each other, and then drank to cement the temporary partnership.

***

When the miners began to fill the saloon, Clint was on the lookout for both Benny Diamond and Big Jack Hunter. He was still sitting with Parker, nursing the last of a few beers.

"There's Jack," he said.

"Which one?" Parker asked.

"The big one."

Big Jack was with three other miners, laughing and back-slapping. When he looked around and saw Clint, he said something to the others, grabbed his beer and walked over.

"There you are!" he said, loudly. "Who's yer friend?"

"This is—" Clint started, but Parker interjected quickly.

"Butch."

"Hiya, Butch," the big miner said. "Big Jack Hunter."

The two men shook hands and Jack sat down.

"Did you find out anythin' today?" he asked Clint.

"Just one thing."

"What was that?"

"I heard stories about miners trying to steal from other miners' claims."

Jack stopped with his beer halfway to his mouth.

"Who tol' ya that?"

"It doesn't matter," Clint said. "Is it true?"

"That's a story told by people who hate miners," Jack said. "We're all hard workers."

"So you're saying it's not possible that somebody did something to Benny in order to steal his claim?"

"I'm sayin' if somebody hurt Benny," Jack said, "it wasn't another miner."

"Who, then?"

"I dunno," Jack said. "But there are folks around here who ain't miners, who don't wanna do the work, but who want the gold. I think maybe you oughtta look for some of them." With his beer in hand, stood up quickly. "I'm gonna go back to my friends."

"Do you think your friends would talk to me?" Clint asked.

"I think you better ask 'em yerself."

As the big miner went back to the bar, Clint had the feeling he wasn't going to get any more help from Big Jack Hunter.

Chapter Eighteen

"That's the fella who was helpin' you?" Parker asked.

"He was," Clint said. "I don't think he will be anymore. In fact . . ."

"What?"

"Maybe he wasn't helping me, at all."

"Whatayamean?"

"I mean," Clint said, "maybe he wasn't trying to help me. Maybe he was trying to distract me."

"So now you're thinkin' he may have had somethin' to do with your friend's disappearance?"

"Could be," Clint said, "but I'll have to talk to some of the other miners before I make up my mind."

"And when do you wanna start?" Parker asked.

"No time like the present," Clint said.

He stood up and walked to the bar where Big Jack was standing with his friends. Parker rose and followed him. Big Jack saw him coming, stopped laughing and drew himself up to his full height.

"You fellows mind if I ask you a few questions?" Clint said.

"About what?" Jack asked.

"I'm sure you've told them already, Jack," Clint said. "Have any of you seen Benny Diamond, lately?"

"Just at his mine," one of them said, "you know, when we walk by."

"And when did you see him last?" Clint asked.

A couple of them just shrugged, but the one who had spoken said, "Probably a couple of days ago."

"At his mine?"

"Yeah, I think so." The other three looked at him. "Uh, I ain't sure."

"Okay," Clint said, "thanks."

He and Parker went back to their table.

"Whataya think?" Parker asked.

"Somebody's holding something back," Clint said. "The others didn't want him talking to me."

"So whataya gonna do?"

"I'll have to get him alone, without anyone else to hear what he tells me."

"But you don't even know his name."

"Don't worry," Clint said, "I'll find out."

"Not from a miner," Parker predicted.

"I noticed the bartender was listening to our conversation."

"And you think he'll tell you the name?" Parker asked. "He doesn't seem to be the talkative type."

"He may not tell me," Clint said, "but I know a couple of people he might tell."

Parker knew exactly who he was referring to.

"You hungry?" Clint asked Parker.

"I could eat."

"Let's go someplace more quiet."

***

When Clint and Parker went back to their table, Big Jack turned and leaned on the bar. The other three followed. He gave the bartender a hard look until the man walked away.

"Remember what he said," Big Jack told the others. "Nobody talks to Adams." He glared at the man who had spoken to Clint. His name was J.P.

"I didn't tell him nothin'," J.P. said. "Just that I saw Benny."

"Nothin' means nothin', J.P.," Big Jack said. "You got it?"

"Yeah, yeah, I got it."

Jack went back to talking to all three of the other men.

"Pass it around the mountain," he said. "Nobody talks to Clint Adams about Benny Diamond."

The three of them nodded.

Big Jack motioned for the bartender to come over. "Fresh beers for everybody," he said.

***

Clint and Parker went to the first cafe Clint had eaten in when he arrived in town.

"You fellas are gettin' to be regulars," the waiter said. "What can I get you?"

"Steak," Clint said.

"Chicken," Parker said.

"Right away."

"So you've been here before," Clint said.

"Ain't too many places to eat in town, and that other café's full of miners."

"That's a good point," Clint said. "Maybe I should eat there tomorrow night."

"Tell me, Clint, what kinda guy is this friend of yours, Benny?"

"Well, to me he was always a friendly little guy who liked to talk," Clint sad. "What I'm gettin' since I got here is that he doesn't talk to anyone."

"So he's changed?"

"Or somebody's lying."

"From what you say," Parker commented, "I'm gettin' the feelin' a lot of lyin' goes on around here."

"Yeah," Clint said, "I'm afraid I'm getting the same feeling."

Chapter Nineteen

"Why don't you use your gun?" Parker asked.

They were eating their supper, discussing different ways to go in the search for Benny Diamond.

"Use my gun how?" Clint asked.

"Threaten people," Parker said. "Point your gun in their face and make 'em talk to you."

"First of all," Clint said, "I don't take my gun out unless I'm going to use it. Second of all—well, there is no second. I don't do that."

"Not even to save your friend?"

"Oh, I get it," Clint said. "You used your gun to save your friend."

Parker touched the pistol he had tucked into his belt and said, "Yeah, I did."

"If I had to use my gun to save Benny's life, I would," Clint said. "But I don't threaten people. Not usually, anyway."

"Well," Parker said, "I hope talkin' to them will get you what you want."

"So do I," Clint said, "because I don't want to have to start shooting miners."

"I know," Parker said, "you'll only do that if they start shootin' at you. But they're miners. What if they come at you with axe's or hammers?"

"If they use their weapons," Clint said, "I'll use mine."

"That's good to know."

"You told me the buyer shot your friend, and then you shot him."

"That's right."

"When you drew, he already had his gun in his hand?"

"Yeah," Parker said, "I had to act fast."

"I guess you did," Clint said.

"I did it without thinkin'."

"That's good," Clint said. "That shows you've got good instincts. You need those to stay alive."

"Yours must be pretty good for you to be alive this long," Parker said.

"This long?" Clint said. "I'm not ancient."

"You've lived a long time for somebody with your reputation."

"Well, that much is true."

They finished their meal, and Clint paid because he thought he must have more money than Parker. After all, he and his partner had not been paid for their delivery.

Outside Clint said, “We’ll have to wait until morning to go up the mountain and question the miners at their claims, rather than all together in a saloon.”

“In the saloon they’ll be drunk enough to give you trouble,” Parker said, “so that sounds like a good idea.”

Clint looked at Parker’s Colt, stuck in his belt.

“Meanwhile, since you’re going to be watching my back,” Clint said, “why don’t I buy you a holster?”

“I ain’t gonna argue with that,” Parker said.

***

They went to the mercantile store, where Clint found a holster and bought it for Parker. The young man strapped it on immediately and dropped his gun into it. Then he drew it and holstered it a few times.

“Feels good,” he said. “Thanks, Clint.”

With the saloons full of liquored up miners, they decided not to go back to the Golden Nugget. There was a smaller saloon Clint hadn’t gone to yet, so he decided they should take a look at that one. It was down a side street and had a sign over the door that just said SALOON. A quick look over the batwing doors showed it to be almost empty, and the men inside were not miners.

"This should do for a beer," Clint said, and they entered.

The bartender was a bored looking man who had been half-dozing while leaning on the bar. He straightened up as they approached. There were three other men, seated at tables. One was middle-aged, alone, his head hanging over a half-filled beer mug. The other two were old-timers, playing poker for match sticks.

"What can I getcha?" he asked.

"Two beers," Clint said.

"Sure thing."

He drew the beers and set them on the bar.

"You ever get any miners in here?" Clint asked.

"Once in a while," the bartender said, "but they mostly go to the Nugget."

"Yeah, we were there," Parker said. "Pretty crowded with 'em."

"Just as well," the bartender said. "I don't need their kind here."

Clint looked around.

"Looks like you need somebody in here," he said.

"I do okay off the locals here in town," the bartender said. "Don't really like the miners that much."

"None of us do," the middle-aged man at the table said.

"That's for sure," one of the poker players added.

"Do the miners give the locals a lot of trouble?" Clint asked.

"Oh, they think because they're takin' gold outta the mountain, they own the place," the bartender said.

"Isn't their gold keeping the town going?" Parker asked. "I mean, they come down here and spend it, don't they?"

The other poker player looked up and said, "Lad, we'd be doin' just fine without them."

"Folks around here don't need much," the bartender said. "That Golden Nugget opened up to cater to the miners. It used to just be this place, and we did fine."

"So the locals come here, and the miners go to the Nugget," Clint said. "Sounds like the only time the two mix is when the miners spend their gold."

"That's about it," the barman said.

"Do you know any of the miners?" Clint asked.

"One or two of them are all right," the bartender said.

"Do you know Benny Diamond?" Clint asked.

"Benny? Sure. Benny's okay. He's not like the others."

"What makes him so different?" Clint asked.

"For one thing," one of the poker players said, "he's our age."

Clint turned and looked, saw the three men looking at him and nodding.

"So you all know Benny?" he asked.

"Sure, we do," the man seated alone said.

"Have any of you seen him lately?"

"Not for a few days," the lone man said.

"Not lately," the poker players said.

"You a friend of his?" the bartender asked.

"Yes, and I've been looking for him," Clint said. "I think he's missing."

"Really?" the man said. "You tried his mine?"

"I was up there, and it's kind of a mess. Big Jack Hunter took me there."

"Jack Hunter?" one of the poker players said, scowling.

"He took you to Benny's mine?" the lone man asked.

"Yeah, he did. Why?"

"Benny hates Big Jack," the other poker player said.

"Well," Clint said, "Big Jack sure as hell didn't tell me that. Do you know why?"

"Hunter's been after Benny's mine," the bartender said. "Benny used to come in here and complain about Hunter tryin' to buy him out."

"This has got real interestin', ain't it?" Parker asked.

"It sure has," Clint said.

Chapter Twenty

"Looks like I've got to talk to Big Jack again," Clint said.

"I wouldn't do that in the Golden Nugget, if I was you," the bartender said. "Those miners are a close group."

"All of 'em?" Parker asked.

"Not all," the bartender said, "but you gotta watch the bunch that're controlled by Big Jack."

"No wonder he acted so helpful when we first met," Clint said.

"He's already taken over three other mines," one of the poker players said.

"And what's the sheriff doing about it?" Clint asked.

"Nothin'," the lone man said. "He just sweeps out his stable."

"He ain't a real lawman," the bartender said, "just somebody they stuck a badge on."

"What happened to the miners after Big Jack took over their claims?" Clint asked.

"Two of them are still workin' the mine, but for Hunter," the barman said.

"And the third one?" Parker asked.

"He ain't been seen in a long time."

Clint and Parker exchanged a glance.

"Might not do you any good to talk to the other miners," Parker said.

"Or," Clint said, "I can talk to the two Big Jack bought out." He looked at the bartender.

"Bought out is a nice way of puttin' it."

"Do you know their names, or the names of their mines?"

"Lemme see . . ." The Bartender rubbed his jaw, then looked over at his customers. "Come on, you fellas. What're their names?"

The man sitting alone said, "One is Anton Dowler. He came to this country from somewhere overseas to get rich. He thought he had until he ran into Big Jack. He named his mine after some woman he knew back home, but I think Hunter changed it."

"And the other one?" Clint asked.

One of the poker players looked over.

"Graham Stevens," he said. "The mine was called 'Graham's Acre.' Think it still might be."

Clint looked at Parker, who said, "Got it."

"Dowler and Stevens, they drink at the Nugget?"

"To tell you the truth," the bartender said, "I ain't seen them in a while, I don't think Hunter even lets them come down from that mountain."

Parker looked at Clint.

"How do we get up there to talk to them when Hunter ain't around?" he asked. "We don't wanna try to get up there at night."

"I've been up there once," Clint said. "I think I can do it again."

"In the dark?"

Clint shrugged.

"Unless," he said, "we come up with a better idea."

Chapter Twenty-One

Big Jack moved his men to a table in the back of the Golden Nugget.

"Drinks?" Dixie asked, coming over.

"Five beers," Jack said.

"Comin' up."

"Who was that young feller with the Gunsmith?" John York asked.

"I don't know," Jack said, "but I'd like to find out, before anythin' comes to a head."

"Whataya mean?" one of the other men asked.

"Well, Adams ain't gonna stop lookin' for Benny," Jack said. "We've gotta be prepared for what he's gonna do."

"We can't go up against the Gunsmith with guns," another man said.

"I know that," Jack said. "I just wanna know if we're gonna have to go against him alone, or with help."

"From that boy?"

"Billy the kid was a boy," Jack said. "And this kid is wearin' a gun."

"What's he doin' here?" York asked.

"Whataya mean?" Jack asked.

"I mean Adams is here lookin' for Benny, but what's the kid doin' here?"

"Good question," Jack said. "Let's find out, tomorrow." He looked at one of the other men. "Eddie, you do it."

"Me?" Eddie said. "How?"

"Just ask questions," Jack said. "I wanna know by the end of the day."

"Who do I ask?" Eddie said.

"Anybody," Jack said, "and everybody. Don't screw it up."

"Yeah," Eddie said, still unsure, "okay."

Big Jack looked, suddenly aware that Dixie had been standing there with a tray of beers.

"Thanks, Dixie," he said. "You can put 'em down."

"Right," she said, setting the glasses down on the table and then walking away.

"Drink up," Jack said. "We're goin' back up to the mine tonight. All except you, Eddie. Spend the night here and start askin' your questions in the mornin'."

"Spend the night? Where?"

"Figure it out," Big Jack said.

The others laughed.

***

Clint and Parker had another beer each before they left the saloon.

"My name's Rollo," the bartender said. "Come back in here anytime."

"Thanks, Rollo," Clint said, then turned and added, "and thanks to you all. You've been very helpful."

"We hope you find Benny," one of the poker players said.

"I'll find him," Clint said, "or find out what happened to him. You can be sure of one or the other."

Clint and Parker left the saloon and walked to their hotel.

"I have to check on Foreman before I turn in," Parker said, as they crossed the small lobby and walked past the desk.

"I'm at the end of the hall," Clint said. "I'll walk with you."

As they went up the steps Parker said, "Looks like we're both tryin' to help friends who got themselves into trouble."

"At least we know where your friend is," Clint said, "and he's been treated by a doctor."

"I hope when we find your friend," Parker said, "that's all he needs."

"I hope so, too."

When they reached Foreman's room they stopped, and Parker unlocked the door. He peered in, saw that the man was sleeping, breathing deeply. He closed and locked the door.

"I was supposed to bring him some more food," Parker said. "He probably went to sleep hungry. I'll have to make it up to him by bringin' him a big breakfast."

"A good one, from the café," Clint suggested.

"Yeah."

"Why don't we have breakfast there, and then you can bring his back."

"Sounds good," Parker said.

They reached his room, and he unlocked the door.

"Thanks again for the holster," he said.

"A proper gun needs a proper holster," Clint said. "That looks like a nice Colt."

"It's a good gun," Parker said, "but I'd like a newer one, some time." Then he realized how that sounded. "I—I didn't mean I want you to buy me one."

"That's okay," Clint said. "I didn't think you were hinting. Let's both get some sleep. I think we need it."

"'night," Parker said, and went into his room.

Clint walked down to his own room and entered. He lit the oil lamp by his bed, hung his gunbelt on the bedpost, and removed his boots. Before he could remove his clothes, however, he fell asleep.

Chapter Twenty-Two

Clint woke the next morning with renewed purpose. He now knew that Big Jack Hunter was the enemy. Now he needed to find out just how bad an enemy he was. He also needed to know how much backing he had.

He met Parker in the lobby, and they walked to the café for breakfast.

"Did you check on your friend, this morning?" Clint asked.

"He was still asleep, which I guess is good. The doctor said he needs a lot of rest. I'll wake him when I bring him his breakfast."

When they reached the café, they found only a few tables taken by locals. They took a table toward the back.

"'mornin', gents," the waiter said. "What can I getcha?"

"Steak-and-eggs for me," Clint said.

"Bacon-and-eggs," Parker said.

"Coffee for you both?"

They nodded.

"Comin' up."

The waiter went to the kitchen, Clint and Parker looked around. They were drawing no looks from the other diners.

"These locals ain't very curious, are they?" Parker asked.

"I guess not."

"You know, when I got here, I didn't notice there was a locals versus miners thing goin' on."

"I didn't either," Clint said. "I was just interested in finding Benny, but now I've had my eyes opened."

The waiter came with the coffee and breakfasts at the same time, and they dug in.

***

After eating they walked back to the hotel so Parker could bring Foreman a plate. He was awake and happy to see the food.

"Earl, this is Clint Adams."

Around a mouthful of bacon-and-eggs the man said, "Gladda meet ya."

"Hope you're feeling better," Clint said.

"Now that I'm eatin', yeah," Foreman said. "What are you fellas doin'?"

"Clint's got a friend here who's a miner, and he's tryin' to find him. I'm helpin'."

"Good for you," Foreman said. "At least you got somethin' to do." He munched on a piece of bacon. "I should be ready to ride in a day or two."

"I think we'll let the doc decide that, Earl," Parker said. "I can have 'im come over here and look at ya, maybe tomorrow mornin'."

"That's fine."

"Well, just finish your breakfast and leave the cup and plate on the floor. I'll fetch 'em back to the café later," Parker said.

"Thanks, Butch," Foreman said. "But you two boys better be careful of the miners, though. They're kind of a close-knit group."

"How do you know that?" Clint asked. "Have you been here before?"

"No, but I've been in my share of mining towns," Foreman said. "They band together."

"I think that's what we've been finding out," Clint said.

He and Parker left the room and went back downstairs.

"So what's first?" Parker asked.

"Those mines that Big Jack took over," Clint said. "We've got two names."

"Graham Stevens and Anton Dowler," Parker said.

That surprised Clint.

"You've got a good memory."

"Yeah, for some things. So we're goin' up the mountain?" Parker asked anxiously.

"That's probably where we're going to find them," Clint pointed out.

"We'll have miners all around us."

"That's true," Clint said. "We'll just have to keep our eyes open."

"Watch each other's back."

"You've got it," Clint said.

They headed down the street, out of town and to the base of the mountain path.

"This place is like a ghost town durin' the day," Parker said, looking back.

"I guess the locals are seeing to their business indoors," Clint said.

Parker gazed up the path.

"You sure you know where you're goin'?"

"Up to a point," Clint admitted. "Let's just see what happens."

"Lead the way, then," Parker said.

"Just walk where I walk," Clint said.

"Count on it," Parker said.

***

Eddie Granger spent the morning asking questions, stopping into the mercantile, the cafes and the hotel. It all led him to the doctor, and when he finally had the answers Big Jack wanted, he started up the mountain.

Chapter Twenty-Three

"This is Benny's mine," Clint said.

"Did you look inside?" Parker asked.

"Yeah, but we better do it again, just in case I missed something," Clint said.

"Sure."

The area outside the mine entrance hadn't been touched. There were still tools strewn about, and a cold fire. Inside Clint grabbed an oil lamp and lit it, then led the way. He couldn't see that anything had changed since the last time he was there.

"I don't see how they can do this, day-in, day-out," Parker said. "I couldn't stand it. What about you?"

"I've done it once or twice, years ago," Clint said, "but this is not the life for me, either."

Parker looked around at the walls and the ceiling.

"Where is it?" he asked.

"What?"

"The gold," Parker said. "I don't see it. I just see . . . rocks."

"It's ore, really," Clint said, "in the walls. It has to be dug out. It takes a lot of work."

"But your friend, he's old, right?"

"Sixty or so," Clint said, "but he's been a miner most of his life. He's got the . . . drive for it. And he's always had the strength. But I haven't seen him in years, so I don't know where he stands, right now."

They walked further in, but then the walls seemed to start closing in on Parker.

"I have to get out of here, Clint," Parker said. "I'm findin' it hard to breathe."

"Yeah, all right," Clint said. "This place isn't telling us anything."

They turned around and headed back.

***

While Clint and Parker were inside Benny Diamond's mine, Eddie Granger walked past the entrance, unaware that anyone was inside. He continued on, heading for Big Jack Hunter's claim, to bring Hunter his news.

***

When Clint and Parker got back outside, they both stopped and took a deep breath.

"Jesus," Parker said. "I don't care if I never go into another mine."

"It's not for everyone," Clint admitted, blowing out the lamp and setting it aside. "Let's go find those other mines, but don't worry, you won't have to go in."

"Fine with me."

***

When Eddie reached Big Jack's mine, he found Jack and the others sitting around the fire, drinking coffee.

"You better have what I asked you for," Jack said, "otherwise, what the hell are ya doin' here?"

"The kid's name is Robert Leroy Parker," Eddie said. "He brought another man into town with a gunshot wound. The doctor patched him up, and he's in a room at the hotel. Parker ain't gonna leave town until his friend is ready to ride."

"Who's the friend?"

"According to the hotel register, his name's Earl Foreman," Eddie said.

"Either name mean anythin' to anybody?" Jack asked.

They all shook their heads.

"Okay then," Jack said, "it looks like we only have one reputation to deal with."

"But it's the Gunsmith," Eddie said.

"I know that," Jack said, "but he ain't gonna intimidate anybody on this mountain. I'm gonna have to talk to a bunch of the others today."

"Whataya want us to do?" Eddie asked.

"What you're supposed to do," Jack said, "You're miners, ain't ya? Get to work."

***

Clint stopped and pointed to the sign that said GRAHAM'S ACRE.

"It should be just up ahead," Clint said.

"As long as I don't have to go in," Parker said.

As they approached the mine, a man came out, pushing a wheelbarrow of ore ahead of him. He was medium height, on the stocky-side, and looked to be in his fifties. When he saw them, he stopped and set the wheelbarrow down.

"Can I help you gents?" he asked.

"My name's Clint Adams. I'm a friend of Benny Diamond. I was wondering if I could talk to you about Big Jack Hunter, Mr. Stevens."

"Graham Stevens, that's right. And you wanna know about Hunter?" Stevens asked. "Not Benny?"

"I know all I need to know about Benny," Clint said. "I just don't know where he is."

“So why do you wanna talk about Big Jack?”

“I heard that Jack’s been taking over other miner’s claims,” Clint said. “I was told he did it to you. I’m wondering if he was trying to do it to Benny.”

“I don’t know where you heard—”

“Look, Stevens,” Clint said. “I don’t care what kind of deal you and Big Jack made. I was told he’s taken over some mines where the previous owners have disappeared. I need to know if he did that to Benny.”

“I don’t know,” Stevens said. “I can’t tell you what happened with other mines. Yeah, he took me over, and now I work for him. But I ain’t disappeared.”

“Mr. Stevens,” Clint said, “what do you know about Jack Hunter and Benny Diamond?”

Stevens frowned.

“I need a drink. You want a drink?”

“No,” Clint said, “but you go ahead.”

Stevens led the way over to a campsite. There was a pot of coffee on the fire, but that wasn’t what he was interested in.

Chapter Twenty-Four

Stevens opened a wooden chest and brought out a bottle of whiskey.

"Since you don't want any, I'll just . . ." he said, and drank straight from the bottle. "Coffee?" he asked.

"No, thanks," Clint said.

"I'll take some water," Parker said.

"Sure." Stevens picked up a canteen and passed it to Parker, who took a swig and passed it back.

"Thanks."

"Are you ready to answer my question, Mr. Stevens?" Clint asked.

"Look," Stevens sad, "all I know is Jack was interested in Benny's mine."

"Why?" Clint asked. "It's such a small operation."

"Sometimes the smallest claim can end up being the richest," Stevens pointed out.

"Is that what happened with Benny?" Clint asked. "Did he hit it rich?"

"Not that I know of," Stevens said, "You'd have to ask Big Jack."

"I'll do that," Clint said. "What do you know about Anton Dowler and his mine?"

"Anton," Stevens said. "He's in the same boat as me. Big Jack took over, and he's makin' Anton keep workin' the mine."

"Where's Dowler's mine?"

"Further up the mountain," Stevens said. "You keep goin' along this path, and then there's one that veers up. Anton is up there."

"Does he work the mine alone?"

"He can't," Stevens said. "He can't get the ore down the mountain alone. Not from how high up he is."

"But you and Benny, you can work alone?"

"Benny and me, we were the only one-man operations on this mountain. Now it might be just me."

"Do you think Anton will talk to me?" Clint asked.

"You said you're Clint Adams, right?"

"That's right."

"The Gunsmith?"

"Right, again," Parker said.

"Then just introduce yourself," Stevens said. "He'll talk to you."

"One more thing, Mr. Stevens."

"It's just Graham."

"Graham," Clint said, "when's the last time you saw Benny Diamond?"

"I'd have to say . . . days ago."

"Where?"

"At his mine," Stevens said. "I was on my way down, saw him, and we waved."

"All right, Graham," Clint said. "Thanks."

"You know," Stevens said, "since you're the Gunsmith, you could probably do me a big favor."

"If I can," Clint said. "What is it?"

"You could kill Big Jack."

***

They stopped at the point where they would have to veer off and go higher to get to Anton Dowler's mine.

"That looks like a climb," Parker said.

"I tell you what, Butch," Clint said. "Why don't you stay here and keep watch while I go up."

"Are you sure?" Parker asked. "Stevens said Anton's got some workers."

"Two or three," Clint said. "I should be okay. Meanwhile, you can keep an eye out."

"For what?" Parker asked. "You're just tryin' to give me an excuse not to go up, ain'tcha?"

"As a matter of fact," Clint said, "I am."

"I'll take it," Parker said.

Chapter Twenty-Five

Clint was out of breath by the time he reached the mouth of Anton Dowler's mine. When he got there, two men, covered with dust and dirt, turned and stared at him. The whites of their eyes shone out of their grimy faces. Neither of them spoke.

"I'm looking for Anton Dowler," he said.

They continued to stare at him. All he could tell was that they were sturdy men. The amount of dirt that covered them made it impossible to guess their ages.

"Anton?" Clint said, again.

One man turned and pointed into the mine.

"Great," Clint muttered.

But as he started toward the mine entrance, the other man put a hand out to stop him, then turned and walked in.

"Is he fetching Anton for me?" Clint asked the remaining man.

The man simply stared.

"Okay," Clint said, "I'll wait."

After a few moments the man returned, leading another. That man stopped at a barrel, dipped a rag into it, and then mopped his face and hands with it. As the grime was washed away, Clint saw a rather dour looking man in his forties.

Once his hands and face were relatively clean, he took a drink of water, then turned to Clint.

"You lookin' for me?"

"I am if you're Anton."

"I am Anton."

"My name's Clint Adams. Can we talk?"

"What does the Gunsmith want to talk to me about?" Anton asked.

"Benny Diamond," Clint said, "And Big Jack Hunter."

Anton thought a moment, then turned to his men and said, "Keep working."

He led Clint off to one side and around a corner. There stood a shack, with a fire going outside of it.

"I'm having a whiskey," Anton said. "Do you want one?"

"After that climb up here, I think I need one," Clint said. "Thanks."

"I'll be right back," Anton said, and went into the shack.

He was there a few minutes, so Clint thought he better play it safe. He walked over to the shack and stood with his back against the wall.

The front door opened, and Anton came out with a bottle of whiskey in one hand and a pistol in the other. He stopped when he didn't see Clint.

"I'm right here," Clint said.

Anton turned, and his eyes widened as Clint snatched the gun from his hand.

"What's this for?"

"I was just . . . being safe," Anton said. "After all, you kill people, don't you?"

"Not today," Clint said. "Here, if it makes you feel better." He handed the gun back. "You mind?" he indicated the whiskey bottle.

Anton handed it over, and Clint took a swig, handed it back. Anton stuck the gun in his belt and took a drink.

"What's on your mind?" he asked Clint.

"I've been trying to find Benny Diamond," Clint said. "He's a friend of mine."

"Is he missing?" Anton asked.

"Seems to be."

"Come sit by the fire."

They walked over and sat. Clint pulled his jacket closer around him. If he kept coming up this mountain, he was going to need a heavier coat.

Anton held the bottle out again, but Clint looked at the coffee pot on the fire.

"I think I'd rather have a cup of coffee."

"Help yourself."

Clint looked around, found a tin cup that looked fairly clean, and filled it. The coffee was black and strong and warmed his insides.

"I suppose you better tell me why you are here," Anton said.

"Big Jack Hunter," Clint said.

"What about him?"

"I know he's taken over your claim, and he's making you work for him."

"Who told you that?"

"I just came from Graham Stevens."

"Oh."

"I need to know if Big Jack's done something to Benny."

"Something?"

"Killed him?" Clint said. "Sent him off somewhere. Taken over his claim?"

Anton studied Clint for a moment, then took another drink from the bottle.

"Big Jack would kill me for talking to you," he said.

"I'm not going to tell him," Clint said. "Not about you or Stevens. In fact, I mean to talk to other miners, too."

"They won't talk to you," Anton said. "Not if Jack tells them not to."

"Does he own the damn mountain?"

"He's trying to," Anton said. "He's been trying to take Benny's claim, but Benny won't let him."

"And now Benny's missing."

"I didn't know that," Anton said.

"Have you seen Benny lately?"

"I don't go down the mountain," Anton said.

"What about supplies?"

"I send one of the men," Anton said. "I like it up here. I may not own it anymore, but I like it."

"There's another mine Big Jack's taken over, isn't there?" Clint asked.

"Yeah," Anton said, "and it's even further up the mountain."

"Who did he take that one from?" Clint asked.

"A fella named Walter Sellig," Anton said.

"And is Sellig working it for him?"

Anton looked around, as if someone might hear what he was saying.

"No, he's . . . gone."

"Gone?" Clint said. "Did he leave, or are you saying he's dead?"

"Can't say I really know."

"Anton, did you sell out to Big Jack because you thought he'd kill you if you didn't?"

"Maybe," Anton said. "I think I sold out because I'm a coward. Maybe I was afraid to find out the answer to that question."

"Do you think he killed Sellig?"

"Maybe."

"And do you think he'd kill Benny?"

"He might," Anton said.

"I suppose I'm just going to have to ask him." Clint stood. "Thanks for talking to me."

"Can I give you some advice?"

"Sure."

"If you go against Big Jack, he'll have a lot of men behind him. More than you can kill with a six-gun. You better have some extra fire power."

"I do," Clint said. "I've got extra guns, and another man to back me."

"Just two of you?" Anton asked. "Against this mountain? If I was you, I'd make sure you go up against Jack in town, and not up here."

"Now that," Clint said, "does sound like good advice."

Chapter Twenty-Six

Clint went back down to where Parker was waiting, his arms wrapped around himself in an attempt to ward off the cold.

"Any chance we can go someplace warmer?" he asked Clint.

"Yeah," Clint said, "we're going back down. I think I found out what I need to know."

"Which is?"

"Big Jack's the only one who can tell us what happened to Benny."

"So we're gonna ask 'im?"

"We're definitely going to ask him," Clint said. "But let's go back to town first and get warm."

"Thank God."

***

When they got back to town, it was simply warmer because they weren't up on the mountain.

"It ain't even Winter," Parker said. "Whatta they do up there when it is?"

"My guess is it gets pretty warm inside the mines," Clint commented.

They went directly to the café where they each ordered a bowl of soup.

"You fellas are really keepin' us in business," the waiter said. "Just lemme know if ya want anythin' else."

"Thanks," Clint said.

"So," Parker said, "what now?"

"Eat your soup," Clint said.

***

For the rest of the afternoon, Big Jack went around to the mines to talk to the other miners to see who he could count on. Since most of them were afraid of him, most of them agreed to back him. When he got back to camp, he told his men.

"Do they know everything?" John York asked.

"They know what I told them," Big Jack said. "That's all they need to know."

"And do they know about the Gunsmith?"

"Oh yeah," Jack said, "but they're more afraid of me than they are of him."

"And that's what you want, ain't it?" York asked.

"You bet your ass," Big Jack Hunter said. "That's exactly what I want."

Chapter Twenty-Seven

Clint and Parker were in the Golden Nugget that night when the miners started to show up.

"You know," Parker said, "if you brace Big Jack here, he's gonna have a lot of friends backin' him up."

"What do I care?" Clint asked. "I've got Butch Parker."

"Uh, that's not exactly the name I wanna go by," Parker said.

"Bob Parker, then?" Clint asked. "Leroy?"

"No," Parker said, "I'm gonna go by the name Butch Cassidy."

"Cassidy?" Clint asked. "Why's that?"

"I had a friend named Mike Cassidy a while, back," Parker said. "He was older, sort of took me under his wing."

"You mean like a mentor?"

"A what?"

"A . . . teacher?"

"Yeah, I suppose."

"And what did he do?" Clint asked.

Parker hesitated, then said, "He was a cattle thief."

"Ah," Clint said, and nothing else.

***

Big Jack sent Eddie on ahead to have a look inside the Nugget.

"He's there," Eddie said, coming back down the street. "Sitting at a table with that young fella, Parker."

"How do you want to play this?" York asked.

"We'll walk in, go up to the bar and see how he wants to play it," Jack said.

"You're gonna let him call the play?" York asked.

"For now," Jack said. "Let's just go in and see what happens."

Big Jack, York, Eddie and two other men entered the Nugget.

***

"There he is," Clint said, "with four others."

"I didn't expect him to come in alone," Parker said.

Clint watched as the five men walked to the bar and made room for themselves. Other miners seemed to shrink away.

"Wow," Parker said, "they really are afraid of him."

"That's the way he wants it," Clint said.

Jackie appeared at the table with a big smile on her face.

"There's my handsome boy," she said. "Two more beers?"

"Yeah," Parker said, "thanks."

"Comin' up."

They watched her flounce off to the bar.

"How are you doin' with Dixie?" Parker asked.

"What do you mean?"

"I mean, have you been with her again?"

"No."

"Will you be with her again?"

"Maybe," Clint said. "Why are you asking?"

"I don't know what to do about Jackie," Parker said. "Do I have to marry her?"

"Because you went upstairs with her once?" Clint asked. "No."

"She ain't a whore," Parker said. "I thought—"

"There's more to women than just being a whore or a wife, Butch," Clint said. "If you want to be with her again, and she wants you, then do it. But there's no reason to get married. That's real old-fashioned thinking."

"Thanks, Clint," Parker said. "That's a real load off my mind."

"When she comes back with the beers, just smile," Clint told him.

"Okay."

***

"Why's he just sittin' there?" York asked. "Why doesn't he come over?"

"Go over and ask 'im," Big Jack said.

"Me?" York said. "I ain't goin' over there."

"Then just shut the hell up and wait," Jack said. "He'll make up his mind."

"Do we even know who he's been talkin' to?" Eddie asked.

"No," Jack said, "but that might be one of the things he has to tell me."

"You told everybody not to talk to him," York reminded him.

"I know I did, but somebody might have," Jack said.

"Like who?" York asked.

"Who knows? Stevens? Maybe Anton?"

York looked surprised.

"They know better than that."

"Not if they think he can help them get rid of me," Big Jack said.

"You think they got the nerve?" York asked.

"I don't know," Jack said, "but maybe we're gonna find out."

Chapter Twenty-Eight

"Okay," Clint said, "you stay here and watch my back."

"From here?"

"You're good enough with your gun to hit someone from here, aren't you?"

"Well, yeah, but—"

"Just keep your eyes open," Clint said. He stood and walked to the bar.

***

"Here he comes!" Eddie said, with something akin to panic in his tone.

"Take it easy," Big Jack said. "Just let me do all the talkin' and watch for my signal."

"What signal?" York asked.

"You'll know," Jack said, and turned to greet Clint.

***

Clint watched as Big Jack turned to face him, with a smile. The men with him looked concerned.

"Comin' over for a beer, Clint?" Jack asked.

"I think you know the answer to that."

"You got somethin' on yer mind?"

"I want to know what you did with Benny Diamond," Clint replied.

"Benny—" Jack started, looking puzzled. "I tried to help you find 'im."

"I think you're the reason he's missing, Big Jack," Clint said. "I want you to tell me where he is, or what you did to him."

"Why do you think I did somethin' to 'im?" the big miner asked.

"Seems you've been taking over other mines. You were after Benny's, but he wouldn't sell."

"Why would I want a small operation like Benny's?" Big Jack asked.

"I don't know," Clint said. "Maybe you heard that Benny hit it big."

Jack looked around.

"Anybody hear that Benny Diamond hit it big?"

All his lackeys either said no, or simply shook their heads.

"Seems nobody here heard anythin' like that, Clint," Jack said. "Where are you gettin' this?"

"Never mind that," Clint said. "Just know that I'm going to find out the truth, Jack. And when I do, somebody's going to pay."

"Is that a threat?"

"It's a promise."

Clint turned his back and walked away, leaving it to Parker to warn him if anyone made a move.

***

"Whataya think of that?" York asked Big Jack. "I mean, him makin' a promise."

"He's tryin' to scare us," Jack said. "Scare *me*, and that's not gonna happen."

"So what do we do now?" Eddie asked.

"Have another beer," Jack said. "Let's see if he tries to keep that promise."

Big Jack turned his back, leaned on the bar, and waved to the bartender.

***

Clint sat back down with Parker.

"What did you say?" the younger man asked.

"I made him a promise," Clint said.

"What promise?"

"To find out what happened to Benny," Clint said. "And if it's something bad, to make somebody pay."

"Do you think he knows you mean him?"

"Oh, he knows."

Clint looked over at Big Jack and his men. They were all leaning on the bar, keeping their backs to him.

"This is going to be a game of cat-and-mouse."

"Whataya mean?"

"You know," Clint said. "Have you ever seen a cat trying to catch a mouse?"

"I don't—probably. Doesn't the cat slap the mouse around with its paw?"

"If he can get close enough," Clint said.

Parker sipped his beer and thought for a few moments before speaking again.

"So . . . who's the cat and who's the mouse?" he asked. "With you and Big Jack?"

"We're just going to have to wait and see, Butch," Clint said.

Chapter Twenty-Nine

Dixie came over to their table with two beers and said to Parker, "You know, Jackie wants to talk to you."

"She does?"

"Yep."

"Where is she?"

"Up in her room," Dixie said. "You can go up."

Parker looked at Clint.

"Go ahead," Clint said. "If anything was going to happen tonight, it would have by now."

"I'll see you in the mornin', then," Parker said.

He stood up and hurried across the floor to the stairs.

"What's that about?" Clint asked Dixie.

She sat across from him, sipped from the beer Parker had left untouched.

"Whataya think?" she asked. "He's a pretty boy. She likes pretty boys."

"Does she want anything from him?" Clint asked. "I mean, anything . . . permanent."

"Oh, God, no," Dixie said. "She wants a poke from a pretty boy, and that's all. Why, does he want somethin'?"

"No," Clint said. "I mean, he's young and inexperienced, but we talked."

"Jackie's young," Dixie said, "but not so inexperienced. I think she'll be good for him."

"I hope they're good for each other."

"How are you doin' lookin' for Benny Diamond?" she asked.

"I think something's happened to him."

"Oh, no," she said. "Somethin' . . . bad?"

"Pretty bad," Clint said.

"Somebody hurt him?"

"Or worse," he said.

"Who would do that?"

"From everybody I've talked to," Clint said, "it sounds like Big Jack Hunter."

Dixie reached her hand out to take Clint's.

"You've gotta watch out for that man, Clint," she said. "He's dangerous."

"Do you know that from first-hand experience?" Clint asked.

"I've seen him beat men half to death," she said.

"And the sheriff never does anything?"

"You've met him," she said. "He ain't much of a sheriff."

"No, I guess not."

"I know your reputation," she said, "but this is Big Jack's territory."

"I understand that," Clint said. "He's got all the miners and I just have Parker."

"Do you think . . ."

"What?"

"Well . . . what if you got Big Jack alone, without his men behind him?"

"Then it'd be me and Jack," Clint said. "That'd be okay. Why?"

"Well, Jack . . . he sort of likes me," she said. "I could lure him up to my room—"

"Uh-uh, no chance," Clint said. "I'm not risking your neck."

"Aw, that's sweet," she said, "but I can take care of myself."

"There's no reason for you to get involved."

"There's one."

"And what's that?"

"I like you," she said, "and I don't wanna see you get hurt."

"Well, I appreciate the thought, Dixie, but the answer's still no."

"How about if I come to your room after work a little later?" she asked. "Is your answer to that no?"

"My answer to that," he said, "is a big yes."

***

He went back to his hotel, and there was a knock a short time later. Even though he was expecting Dixie, he answered the door holding his gun.

"You won't need that for me," she told him, as he allowed her to enter.

"Can't ever be too careful," he said, replacing the gun in the holster hanging on the bedpost.

She walked to the bed and sat on it.

"Your young partner is still with Jackie," she said. "I was able to hear them through the door as I passed."

"Good," Clint said.

"Never mind them," she said. "Let's get to us." She patted the bed next to her. "Come and sit. It's your bed, you know."

He walked over and sat next to her. She was wearing the same skirt and blouse she'd worn to work the Golden Nugget floor.

She put her hand on his leg.

"You know I don't expect anythin' from you after tonight, right?"

"I know," Clint said. "We're both adults."

She squeezed his leg and said, "Get them trousers off, then."

Chapter Thirty

When the Golden Nugget closed, Big Jack and his men started back up the mountain. But as they walked past the hotel, John York had a suggestion.

"Why don't we just go in there and take him while he's asleep?" he asked. "It sure as hell would be safer."

"Sure," Big Jack said, "go ahead, John. Take Eddie with you. Drag the Gunsmith out of bed and out here to the street."

"Well . . ." York said, ". . . I—I meant all of us."

"Any of you others want to go into the hotel and attack the Gunsmith in his hotel room?"

The other men shook their heads and Eddie said to York, "Don't be volunteerin' me for this."

"We've got time," Big Jack said. "Maybe we'll get lucky and he'll grow impatient and leave town."

"You really think he will?" York asked.

"No," Big Jack said, "I don't. Come on, let's get back to camp."

***

Since they were in Clint's hotel room this time, and not her room above the saloon, Clint decided to take his time. First, he undressed Dixie and laid her on the bed, then undressed while she watched.

He slid into bed with her and busied his hands with the curves of her opulent flesh. She, in turn, ran her hands over his chest, then slid one down between his legs, where she grasped him.

He looked down at her hand as she stroked him.

"I'm trying to go slow, here," he said.

She giggled and leaned into him.

"And I want to go fast!"

"All right," he said, sliding one hand down between her legs, "you can have it your way, for now."

He busied his hand until she was moaning and sopping wet, then mounted her and drove his hard penis home. He fulfilled her request and took her quickly, almost brutally . . .

Later she gave in to his request, and they made love more slowly, so he could enjoy every inch of her body. By the time they were done, she was gasping for air as they lay side-by-side.

"You are a talented man," she said. "I knew that before, but I didn't know how talented."

"And you," he said, "are more than a handful, aren't you?"

"Am I too much to handle?" she asked, playfully.

"Not for me," he said. "You're just right."

She snuggled closer to him.

"Then how would you feel about me spendin' the night here?" she asked. "I really don't want to walk back to my own room tonight."

"I wouldn't mind that at all," he said.

With her head on his left shoulder, they fell asleep, and remained that way until morning . . .

***

In the morning they woke and made love slowly once again.

"I don't believe I've ever been with a man as naturally gentle as you," she said, later.

"Not too gentle, I hope," he said.

"Gentle by nature," she said, "but brutal when I asked you to be. Most men are the other way around—brutal by nature, and gentle only when it's forced on them."

"How can you force a man to be gentle?" he asked.

"I'm not a whore by any means, but I've been with my fair share of men," she said. "And usually, I have to withhold sex before they'll consent to be gentle. And more often than not, it wasn't worth the bargain."

They rose from the bed and dressed.

"Will you have breakfast with me?" he asked.

"I don't think so," she said. "I'm in the same clothes I wore yesterday. I need to wash and change. I'll have breakfast myself after that. You go ahead." She placed her hand on his belly. "I'll wager I've made you a hungry man."

"Starved," he said.

They left the room and in the hall she said, "I'll go out the back way. Come and see me at the Nugget again, if you want to."

"I will," he promised.

She kissed him and hurried to the back stairway.

He went down through the lobby and headed for the café. When he got there, he saw Parker at a table, drinking coffee.

"Have you ordered?" he asked, joining him.

"Just now."

"Hungry?"

"Starving," Parker said. "I never knew being with a woman could make you so hungry in the mornin'."

"A hard night's work usually stirs up an appetite," Clint said.

"Were you with Dixie?"

"I was."

"Jackie likes her a lot," Parker said.

Clint grinned and said, "That makes two of us."

Chapter Thirty-One

Both Clint and Parker had a huge breakfast that consisted of steak-and-eggs and flapjacks, as well as a basket of hot biscuits.

"How's Foreman?" Clint asked.

"He's almost ready to ride," Parker said. "I'll bring him some food today, but then he wants to get out of that room."

"Good for him."

"What about you?" Parker asked. "Has it ever occurred to you just to leave?"

"I can't do that," Clint said. "I have to find out what happened to Benny."

"Well," Parker said, "Earl's reliable. We can recruit him to help me back you up."

"That'd be up to him, Butch," Clint said, "but I can't see why he'd want to do that."

"Are you kiddin'?" Parker asked. "You're the Gunsmith. That's reason enough."

Clint thought that might be reason enough for someone as young as Parker, but not a man like Earl Foreman, who had already been shot at least once.

"Well, you can ask 'im yourself," Parker said, "or I can."

"He doesn't even know me, Butch," Clint said. "If you want, you can ask him. Maybe you'll feel better about backing me, with him backing you."

"I'll talk to 'im when I bring 'im his breakfast."

They both attacked their plates then, and finished breakfast. When they were almost done Parker had the waiter put together a plate for Foreman. He and Clint carried it back to the hotel.

"I'll wait down here," Clint said. "When you come back down, I want to go and have a talk with that sometime sheriff."

"I don't even like sometime law," Parker joked. "I'll just tag along and keep quiet."

He took the plate of food upstairs.

***

When he entered the hotel room, Foreman was sitting up with his feet on the floor.

"Whataya doin', Earl?" Parker asked.

"Just seein' if I can get my feet under me," Foreman said. "I think I can get outta this hotel room tomorrow."

"Let me get the doc over here today to check you over," Parker said. "Meanwhile, I brought you some flapjacks."

"That's great," Foreman said, "but they won't hold me all day."

"I know, I know," Parker said. "Look, I promise I'll bring you some supper later."

Foreman accepted the plate and said, "I'm just sayin' . . ." He uncovered the tray. "Ah, plenty of syrup—and coffee! Good boy." He grabbed the fork and started eating.

"I got somethin' to ask you, Earl."

"Go ahead."

Parker explained about Clint looking for Benny Diamond, and how Parker had agreed to back his play.

"But there are a lot of miners," he went on. "I'm thinkin' if the doc gives you the okay and you can get to your feet, that you could back me while I back him."

"Why would you wanna get involved in the Gunsmith's business?" Foreman asked.

"Well . . . because he's the Gunsmith," Parker said. "Besides, I didn't have much else to do."

"Look, if I get the okay to ride, I think we oughtta get out of here before somebody finds Winston's body and comes lookin'."

"That ranch is pretty tucked away," Parker said. "Nobody's gonna find 'im for a while."

"Still . . ."

"Look, Earl," Parker said, "I already gave my word to Clint I'd back 'im. I have to stay, but you don't. If the doc gives you the okay, and you wanna leave, I'll understand."

"Naw, naw," Foreman said, "if you really wanna do this, I'm in. I ain't gonna leave without ya, Butch."

"That's great!" Parker said. "I'll go and talk to the doc right now."

He hurriedly left the room.

***

Parker rushed downstairs and told Clint about his conversation with Foreman.

"We can stop off and see the doc before we go to the livery to talk to the sheriff," Clint offered.

"That sounds good," Parker said.

They left the hotel and walked over to the doctor's office. Clint remained outside while Parker went inside and talked to the man.

"How'd it go?" Clint asked, when Parker came out moments later.

"Doc's gonna go over and have a look at Earl this mornin'," Parker said.

"Okay, Good. Now let's get over to that livery so I can talk to that part-time sheriff."

Chapter Thirty-Two

Clint and Parker entered the livery stable together. Sheriff Bates Monroe was in the rear, working on a pile of hay with a pitchfork.

"Adams," he said. "You still in town?"

"You know I am, Sheriff," Clint said. "You still have my horse here."

"So I do," Monroe said, leaning on the pitchfork. "And who's this?"

"Butch Cassidy," Clint said, giving the lawman Parker's preferred name. "He's a friend of mine."

"So what can I do for ya?"

"Benny Diamond is missing," Clint said. "I'm sure of that now."

Monroe shrugged.

"What can I do?"

"Well," Clint said, "you're the law. Shouldn't you be out looking for him?"

"You already know I ain't no real lawman, Adams," Monroe said. "Just some poor bastard they stuck a badge on so somebody had the job. But this—" he said, lifting the pitchfork "—is what I do."

"So you're not concerned?"

"I don't usually get involved with the miners, Adams," Monroe said. "Occasionally I'll arrest a drunken local, but that's about it."

"What do you know about Big Jack Hunter?"

Monroe tapped the ground with the pitchfork.

"I know enough not to get in his way," he said.

"Do you know he's taken over other claims?"

"What happens on the mountain is between the miners," the part-time lawman said. "Look, Adams, I told you, I don't get involved with them."

"So if I get involved, I'm on my own."

"I assume that's why you have this young gent with you," Monroe said. "To back your play."

"I just want to know where I stand with the law," Clint said, "if push comes to shove."

"I'd say you should do whatever you want to, Adams," Monroe said. "After all, that's who you are, ain't it? A man who does what he wants?"

"I'm a man who does what he has to, Sheriff," Clint said. "There's a difference."

***

As Clint and Parker were walking away from the livery, the young man said, "Well, that's the most useless lawman I've ever seen."

"And he's not ashamed of it," Clint said.

"It's obvious he's afraid of the miners," Parker said, "and Big Jack, in particular."

"So he takes his sheriff's pay and stays out of the miner's business."

"And with no law to answer to, they do what they want," Parker said.

"Wait a minute," Clint said. "Law."

"What about it?"

"In any mining operation, there's usually a miner's court," Clint said. "They do tend to mind their own business."

"So when a miner breaks the law, other miners judge him?" Parker asked.

"That's the way it usually works."

"But . . . who's in charge?"

"That's also up to the miners," Clint said. "And it's going to take a miner to answer the question."

"So we're goin' back up the mountain?" Parker asked.

"That we are, Butch."

***

They went up as far as Graham Stevens' claim, where they stopped. Stevens was coming out of the mine, covered with dust.

"Mr. Adams," he said. "What brings you back here?"

"A couple of more questions," Clint said. "If you've got the time."

"Just let me get a drink of water to clear my throat," Stevens said.

He walked to a barrel, where he used a cup to scoop some water and drink it.

"All right," he said, "go ahead and ask. What's it about?"

"It's about a miner's court," Clint said. "Is there one, here?"

"There sure is," Stevens said. "Somebody's got to keep the law on the mountain."

"And who presides over the court?" Clint asked.

"That changes, as time goes by," Stevens said.

"Do you suppose you could tell me who presides now?" Clint asked.

"Well," Stevens said, reluctantly, "these days it's Big Jack Hunter."

Chapter Thirty-Three

As Clint and Parker came down off the mountain Parker asked, “So what does that tell us?”

“It might mean that whatever Big Jack did to Benny was approved by the miner’s court.”

“So, does that make it legal?” Parker asked, as they started the walk back to town. “I mean, if he killed Benny and stole his mine?”

“It might be legal to the miners,” Clint said, “but not to me.”

“So it doesn’t change anythin’?”

“No.”

“Now what are you gonna do?”

“I’m going to confront Big Jack and force him to make a move,” Clint said, “because I still can’t prove he did anything to Benny, even though I feel fairly certain he did.”

“So you wanna make him come after you.”

“Yeah, that’s it,” Clint said. “I think that’s my only play.”

“Then you really are gonna need somebody to back you up,” Parker said. “That’ll be me and Earl, if the doc clears ’im.”

"Well, we better find out," Clint said, "then we can make plans."

They headed for the hotel.

***

They entered the room and found Earl Foreman on his feet.

"Just testin' out my legs," Foreman said, as they entered.

"Was the doc here?" Parker asked.

"Yeah, he was," Foreman said. "He said I can walk around, but not ride for a few more days."

"That's it, then," Parker said, looking at Clint. "We're gonna back your play."

"And what is your play, Adams?" Foreman asked.

This was the first time Clint and Foreman had spoken.

"How'd you like to test your legs walking over to the saloon?" Clint relied.

"I thought you'd never ask."

***

They got to the Golden Nugget, grabbed three beers from the bar and took them to a table. At that moment they were the only customers in the saloon.

Clint explained his plan again, this time for Foreman's benefit.

"So, this plan of yours," Foreman said. "Do you think you'll get Big Jack himself to make a try for you, or will he send some of his men?"

"Either way," Clint said, "it'll make it easy for me to go after him."

"And you're sure he did something to your friend," Foreman said.

"Pretty sure," Clint said. "If he comes after me, then I'll be sure."

"Is anybody workin' your friend's mine right now?" Foreman asked.

"We haven't seen anyone the times we've been up there," Clint said.

"If Big Jack took it over, wouldn't he have somebody workin' it?"

"He would," Clint said, "but he might be waiting for me to leave town, first."

That seemed to start Foreman thinking.

"So why don't you?" Foreman asked.

"What do you mean?"

"Leave town," Foreman said, "then, in a few days, sneak back in and see if Big Jack's got somebody in the mine. That'd confirm what you suspect, wouldn't it?"

"You could have a point," Clint said. "And what would you and Butch do while I'm gone?"

"We're just gonna keep our eyes and ears open," Foreman said, "while not pokin' our noses in Big Jack's business. Let him think you're gone."

"I could just camp outside of town," Clint said.

"That'd work," Foreman said. "You'd just have to convince Big Jack that you've given up looking for your friend and left."

"Hmm, the only way I could do that would be to complain loud enough for him to hear it," Clint said.

"Right," Foreman said. "You're givin' up. You could complain here in the saloon later tonight, and also to the sheriff."

"You're just gonna hafta make it real convincin'," Parker said.

"Men usually tell the truth when they're drunk," Clint observed.

"So tonight, the Gunsmith is gonna get good and drunk," Foreman said, "and complain loud enough so everybody can hear him."

Chapter Thirty-Four

Clint began his drunken subterfuge by stopping at the livery stable.

"I hope you ain't here to talk to the sheriff," Bates Monroe said, "'cause I got lots of livery stable business to take care of. The miners are gonna be pickin' up their pack mules today."

"Pack mules?"

"It's the only way they can get their gold ore down the mountain."

"No, I'm not looking for you as sheriff," Clint said. "I just want to check my horse."

"He's in good shape," Monroe said. "You headin' somewhere?"

"Away from here," Clint said. "I'm not making much headway, and I think maybe I might have to give it up. Plus, Big Jack's got a helluva lot of men behind him. I can't really take him on with just a kid to back my play."

"That sounds like a smart idea," Monroe said. "You want me to saddle 'im for ya?"

"Not yet," Clint said. "I might as well keep trying the rest of the day before I give up."

"So where ya headed now?"

"The saloon," Clint said. "I'll have a few drinks while I'm waiting to see if Benny Diamond shows up."

"Seems like you've had a few already," Monroe said.

"I might have to get real drunk to make my final decision to give up the ghost and leave town," Clint said. "It ain't easy for me to quit."

"Sometimes," Monroe said, "it's just the smart thing to do."

Clint touched his nose, closed one eye and said, "I just might be getting close."

He left, hoping Bates Monroe would spread the word.

***

Back in the saloon the locals had started to show up. Clint sat back down with Parker and Foreman and started talking real loud about getting frustrated.

"Maybe," Foreman said, just as loud, "your friend just up and quit his claim."

"That'd be just like the Benny I used to know," Clint replied. "Leave me here looking for him while he's gone off somewhere."

Clint noticed several men turning to look over at him. What he needed, however, was for some of those men to be miners. He decided to leave the saloon and return when the miners were coming in. He couldn't very well make it look like he had been drinking all day. By the time the miners started filing in, he would have to be unconscious.

So he left with Parker and Foreman, staggering a bit to make it look good, and walked back to the hotel. Foreman wanted to lie down for a while, as this was his first day on his feet. But he had a suggestion first.

"Butch, you should go back to the saloon, nurse a beer, and complain about Clint," he said. "Make it seem like you ain't backin' him, anymore."

"That's a good idea," Clint said. "Let's get the word back to Big Jack that Butch is sick of me, and I'm frustrated."

"I could do that."

"Then later tonight," Clint said, "you and me could have a falling out at the Nugget, in front of some of the miners."

"This is all bound to get back to Big Jack," Parker predicted.

"No doubt," Clint said. "Then I'll ride out of town tomorrow, and that'll be that, hopefully."

"Then Big Jack can start workin' your friend's mine," Foreman said.

"I hope so," Clint said. "I just want to catch him doing that."

***

Big Jack Hunter came out of his mine to get some air. He washed his face and hands in a barrel of water, then turned and saw Eddie coming toward him. He'd given Eddie time off from the mine to hang around town and see what he could find out.

"What've ya got?" Jack asked.

"Adams is gettin' frustrated," Eddie said. "He went to the livery to check on his horse, make sure it was in shape to ride. Then he went to the saloon, had a few drinks, and started complainin' about Benny Diamond."

Big Jack rubbed his jaw, thought about what Eddie was telling him.

"If he gives up and leaves town, I'm gonna want you to take some men to Benny's mine and start workin' it. Meanwhile, go back down now with a couple of men and bring up some mules. We're gettin' ready to bring some ore down and get it weighed."

"And Adams?"

"If he's drinking, he'll be in the saloon tonight," Big Jack said. "We'll hear what he has to say then."

Chapter Thirty-Five

Clint stayed in his room until he was fairly sure there were plenty of miners at the Nugget. Also, when he finally walked over there, he didn't sit with Parker and Foreman, but stood at the bar, where his complaining could be easily heard.

At the far end of the bar, Big Jack stood with several of his men.

"Look at Big Jack," Parker whispered to Foreman. "He's takin' it all in."

"Let's hope he's believin' it," Foreman said. "Clint's gonna ride out tomorrow mornin'?"

"That's the plan, thanks to you," Parker said.

"Butch, I was thinkin' maybe we should ride out, too," Foreman said.

"And then come back with Clint?"

"No," Foreman said, "I think we should keep goin'."

"Why?"

"This ain't really our problem is it?" Foreman asked. "Adams is gettin' ready to take on all the miners."

"And you wanna let him do that himself?" Parker asked.

"I'm sure he's useta that," Foreman said. "Butch, we gotta get on with our lives. Remember, we got that bank job—"

"I remember, Earl," Parker said. "But I told Clint I'd back his play. Why don't you go and check out the bank, and I'll catch up—"

"You'll catch up if you're alive," Foreman said. He heaved a huge sigh. "All right, I'll stick this out with you."

They went back to drinking their beer and watching Clint Adams at the bar.

***

"Whataya think, Jack?" John York asked.

"He looks drunk," Jack said, "and he sounds drunk."

"And frustrated," York said.

"And," Big Jack said, "he's not payin' any attention to us."

"That 'cause he's just moanin' about Benny Diamond, and drinkin'," Eddie said.

"And some of the others in here don't like it," Jack said. "Look."

Further down the bar some miners were pointing at Clint, obviously displeased.

"Let's see what happens here," Big Jack said, with interest.

***

Three miners had been listening to Clint complain about Benny Diamond for a couple of hours, and they'd had about enough. Slowly, they moved down the bar until they were standing near Clint.

"That little bastard," Clint said. "He probably left town without telling anybody, and here I am looking for him. How could he just walk away from his claim—"

"All right, that's enough," one of the three miners said. "You can't stand here drinkin' and complainin' about one of us like this. Benny Diamond's a good man."

Clint turned and faced the three miners.

"That's what I thought, too," Clint said, "but it sure looks like he just walked away—"

The miner who was speaking was a big man, and he stuck a thick forefinger into Clint's chest.

"I said that's enough!" he growled. "You don't stand here talkin' about one of us. You ain't a miner, you got no right!"

"And I thank God," Clint said, "I'm not a miner. I'd never want to live that kind of life—"

Two of the miners suddenly grabbed Clint, and the big one punched him in the stomach. They released him and allowed him to sink to the floor.

***

Across the floor Parker started to get to his feet, but Foreman stopped him.

"He knows what he's doin'," the older man said, "and he doesn't want us to interfere."

"Are we just gonna let him take a beatin'?" Parker asked.

"Just watch, Butch," Foreman said.

***

Before another blow could be struck, Big Jack stepped forward.

"Darius!" he snapped. "That's enough!"

"You heard what he's been sayin' about one of us!" Darius shouted.

"I said that's enough," Big Jack repeated. "Back off, all of you."

The other two men obeyed instantly. Darius, a big man himself, stood eye-to-eye with Big Jack for a few moments, but in the end, he backed away.

Jack leaned down and helped Clint to his feet.

"I think you should leave, Adams," he said. "I'm not gonna be able to control these men much longer."

"I'll leave," Clint said, pulling away from Jack drunkenly, "I'll leave this saloon, and this bloody town!"

He staggered to the batwing doors and out. Once outside, he continued to stagger as he made his way to the hotel, sure that someone was watching him from the saloon. He had played his part perfectly.

Chapter Thirty-Six

Parker and Foreman stayed in the saloon a little longer, then went back to their hotel and knocked on Clint's door.

"How did it look?" Clint asked.

"Like everybody believed it," Foreman said. "Especially after you took that punch to the stomach."

"You okay?" Parker asked.

"I'm fine," Clint said. "I'll be riding out early tomorrow, and I'll camp just outside of town."

"We'll keep an eye on what's goin' on," Parker said. "Anything happens you should know about, I can ride out and let ya know."

"Okay," Clint said. "I'll have a small fire going, just so I can make some coffee."

"How are we gonna know if Big Jack is workin' your friend's claim?" Foreman asked. "I ain't in no shape to climb up a mountain."

"Butch?" Clint said.

"Yeah, yeah," Parker said, "I can go up and take a look, see what's goin' on."

"Must be nice to be that young, huh?" Foreman said to Clint.

"I wouldn't remember," Clint said.

"Hey," Parker said, "I can't help it if you guys are old."

"Yeah," Foreman said, "I'm so old I'm goin' to my room to get some sleep."

"I'm staying in my room the rest of the night, too," Clint said.

"Well," Parker said, "I'm gonna go back to the saloon to see what I can hear."

"If it's anything you think I should know, don't worry about waking me up."

"Got it," Parker said.

Foreman and Parker left Clint's room, first peering into the hall to make sure no one saw them. As Parker headed for the stairs, Foreman told him, "Be careful. Don't do anything stupid."

"I ain't stupid, Earl," Parker said, and went down the stairs.

No, Foreman thought, you ain't stupid, just young. It's almost the same thing.

***

Big Jack and his boys were still standing at the bar when Parker walked back into the saloon.

"The kid's back," York said, "and he's alone."

"He didn't make a move to help Adams," Eddie pointed out.

"I noticed that," Big Jack said. "You boys stay right here."

Big Jack got two beers from the bartender, and then walked over to Parker's table.

"Mind if I sit?" he asked.

"Is one of those for me?"

"Sure is."

"Have a seat," Parker said.

Big Jack sat and pushed the beer across the table.

"I hear they call you Butch," the big man said.

"Butch Cassidy," Parker said.

"I thought you were backing Clint Adams," Big Jack said. "Looks like he was standin' alone against those miners."

"Look," Parker said, "He's startin' to get frustrated and I think he's ready to give up. Why should I back him when he ain't even backin' himself?"

"That's a good point," Big Jack said. "What do you think his next move is gonna be?"

"Seems to me he's ready to leave town," Parker said, "but I can't say for sure."

"And what about you?"

"Me? I'm still waitin' for my friend to be ready to ride. Doc says a few more days."

"So you're stayin' because of your friend, not because of Adams."

"I never met Adams before I came here," Parker said. "I thought it'd be excitin' to stand with the Gunsmith—but I don't think he's the Gunsmith I always heard about."

"We all get old," Big Jack said. "You're real young, but you'll find out, eventually."

"Well, while I'm young I plan to live," Parker said. "Seems to me drinkin' and bad-mouthin' miners hereabouts ain't a smart way to go."

"You got that right," Jack said. "You seem like a smart young man."

"And maybe backin' away from Clint Adams is makin' me smarter," Parker said.

"Well," Big Jack said, "it's sure gonna make ya healthier."

"Anyway," Parker said, "thanks for the beer. If you were checkin' to see if I'm backin' away from Clint Adams, the answer's yes."

"Smart boy," Jack said. "Enjoy your beer."

The big miner stood up and returned to the bar. Parker drank the beer, hoping he had been convincing.

Chapter Thirty-Seven

Clint woke early the next morning. Parker hadn't woke him last night, so there was no news. He decided to skip breakfast and just proceed to the livery to saddle his Tobiano and ride out of town. There was no point in checking in with Parker or Foreman, as they knew what his plans were.

When he reached the livery, Bates Monroe was sweeping out one of the stalls.

"Headin' out?" he asked.

"I sure am," Clint said. "I'm tired of this place."

"Want me to saddle your horse?"

"I'll do it myself," Clint said. "I wouldn't want to put you out, Sheriff."

"Hey," Monroe said, "I told you I'm no lawman. The miners run things around here."

"Well, they can run it without me," Clint said.

He walked to the Tobiano's stall and started saddling him.

"Take it easy, Toby," he said. "We'll be out of here in no time."

Monroe leaned on his broom and watched Clint saddle the Tobiano. He followed as Clint walked him outside.

"Fine animal," Monroe said. "Sorry to see him go."

"Well, we're not sorry to leave," Clint said, mounting up. "If anyone asks, tell them I'm glad to be out of here."

"I will," Monroe said.

Clint turned the horse and rode out of town.

***

Since Columbia was located in a box canyon surrounded by mountains, Clint rode to the head of the canyon and came to Bridal Veil Falls, where there were no mining operations. He decided to camp there. He put off unsaddling the Tobiano until he was sure he wouldn't be moving on in a hurry.

He built a fire and put a pot of coffee on. He allowed the Tobiano to drink his fill, then moved him away from the water. After that he sat at the fire and had a cup of coffee while considering his options. They were limited, and in the end, he realized he couldn't do anything for a while—perhaps days—but sit and wait.

***

John York approached Hunter as the big man came out of his shack.

"He's gone," York said.

"What?"

"Adams," York said. "He's gone. Monroe says he rode out this mornin'."

"Did he say where he was goin'?" Jack asked.

"Just that he was glad to be goin'," York said.

"And we're glad he's gone," Jack said. "Get some men together—three, I think—and get them over to the Diamond mine."

"Got anybody in mind?"

"Eddie and two others," Jack said. "Tell Eddie he's in charge."

"You sure about that?" York asked. "Eddie's not that bright."

"That's true, but he's good in a mine, and that's what we need," Jack said.

"Right."

"Oh, York," Jack said, "while you were in town, did you see that kid, Parker?"

"No," York said, "no sign."

"Okay," Jack said, "get Eddie and the others workin'."

"Right away."

Big Jack poured himself a cup of coffee from the fire, satisfied that he'd finally be taking some profit from Benny Diamond's mine.

***

Parker and Foreman had breakfast at the café where the young man had been dining with Clint all week.

"Where's your friend?" the waiter asked.

"This is my friend," Parker said, indicating Foreman. He thought it wise to continue the pretense of separating himself from Clint Adams. "The other man's gone. He's left town."

"I see," the waiter said. "Is this the injured man you've been takin' meals to?"

"He is, and he's feelin' better, so I brought him here."

"Welcome," the waiter said, "what can I get you gents?"

They both ordered ham-and-eggs, flapjacks and coffee. The waiter went off to fetch it.

"That was smart," Foreman said. "The whole town should know that you've backed away from Clint Adams."

"That's what I thought."

The waiter brought them their coffee, and then their plates. There were no other customers in the place.

Over breakfast Foreman asked, "When are you goin' up the mountain to check out that mine?"

"In the afternoon, when the locals and miners are all hard at work," Parker said. "I don't want to take a chance at bein' seen."

"Good thinkin'," Foreman said. "I could go with you—"

"You're not ready for a climb like that," Parker said. "No, you stay at the hotel. Besides, I'll move faster alone."

"You got a point there," Foreman said.

A few other diners entered and took up tables, so Parker and Foreman applied themselves to their breakfasts in silence from that point on.

Chapter Thirty-Eight

Eddie led the two men into the mine, and they got to work. They were leaning into their pickaxes for a short time when one of them said, “My God, what a vein.”

The other man said, “Do you think Benny Diamond found this before—”

“Before what?” Eddie asked, cutting him off.

“I didn’t mean nothin’,” the man said. “I just meant . . . before he left.”

“Why would he leave if he found a vein like this?” the first man asked.

“You two have to stop talkin’,” Eddie said, “and keep workin’, or I’ll have to tell Big Jack you need to be replaced. Is that what you want?”

“Hell, no,” the first man said.

“Don’t tell Jack that,” the second man said.

“Then get to work and keep your mouths shut,” Eddie ordered. “One of you go outside and bring in that wheelbarrow. Jack wants to see profits from this mine right away.”

“Okay,” the first man said, and trotted outside to fetch it.

***

Parker reached the Diamond mine at midday and was able to watch from hiding as a man brought a wheelbarrow out and dumped a load of rocks before going back in again. He left his hiding place to go and look at the rocks, then grabbed one and took it away with him. He hurried back down the mountain.

***

"It's gold," Foreman said.

"Are you sure?"

"Oh, it has to be extracted from the ore," Foreman said, "but if there's more like this, they've got a rich vein."

"Rich enough to kill for?"

"That's for sure," Foreman said.

"Then I've got to get to Clint," Parker said. "He doesn't have to camp out for days."

"Do you know which way he rode?"

"He told me," Parker said. "I'll be able to find 'im."

"Then take that with you and show it to him," Foreman said.

"Stay out of sight, Earl, until I get back," Parker said. "There's no point in pushin' our luck."

"You watch your back, Butch," Foreman said.

Parker took the piece of ore back from his friend and left the room.

***

At the livery, Bates Monroe said, "You leavin' town, too?" while Parker saddled his horse.

"Not til my friend completely recovers from his bullet wound," Parker said. "I'm just gonna give my horse some exercise and get some air myself."

"I'll keep your stall for ya, then," Monroe said.

"Much obliged," Parker said, before riding off.

***

Up in Big Jack's camp, York caught the big man as he came out of the mine for a break.

"Just got word that the kid rode out," he said.

"For good?"

"He said no," York said. "He told Monroe he was just givin' his horse some exercise and wasn't leavin' until his friend's bullet wound healed enough."

"Put somebody in town to keep their eyes open," Big Jack said. "I wanna know what his friend does while he's gone, and when he gets back."

"Right," York said. "And where will you be?"

"Where else?" Jack said. "We've still got plenty of workday ahead of us. Get somebody to town, and then I expect to see you in the mine."

"Right, boss."

***

The man York sent to town was called Quince. He decided the best place for him to keep an eye on the town was from the Golden Nugget Saloon. So he entered, got a beer from the bar, and a table by the front window. He took a long, relaxed breath, enjoying the fact that it wasn't filled with dirt from the mines.

***

Earl Foreman was going stir crazy in his room. Parker had urged him to stay inside, but he didn't see the harm in going out for a drink.

Just one drink.

Chapter Thirty-Nine

Clint heard the horse before he saw it, even over the noise of the falls.

"I could hear you coming," Clint said, as Parker reached his camp.

"I've got somethin' to show you," Parker said, dismounting. "Makes me glad you didn't camp further out of town."

He handed Clint the chunk of ore.

"Where did this come from?" Clint asked.

"Benny Diamond's mine," Parker said. "There are a few men workin' it."

"How did you get it?"

"I just sneaked up and . . . got it," Parker said. "They were dumping piles of it outside the mouth of the mine. They ain't gonna miss one."

"So Benny hit a rich vein," Clint said, "and Big Jack took it away from him."

"And probably . . . what? Killed 'im?"

"I'm going to say yes," Clint said. "Come on, let's get back to town. It's time for Big Jack to pay for what he did."

***

It was dusk when Clint and Parker rode back into town. Clint decided to ride in, bold as brass, instead of trying to sneak in.

The Golden Nugget was alive with light and the sound of rowdy miners. They rode past and dismounted in front of the hotel, tied their horses off and went inside. Parker wanted to let Foreman know they were there.

They went upstairs and knocked on the door of Foreman's room. There was no answer.

"We agreed he was going to stay inside," Parker said.

"Let's force it," Clint suggested.

They both pressed their shoulders to the door, and it popped open. The room was empty.

"Maybe he went out to get something to eat," Clint said. "Or a drink. Let's check the café first, and then we'll go to the saloon."

"Okay."

They left the hotel and walked to the café, which was still open, though empty, except for the waiter.

"Hey, I heard you left town," the man said.

"I'm back," Clint said. "Have you seen our other friend since this morning?"

"No," the waiter said, then looked at Parker and added, "not since he was in here with you."

Clint and Parker looked at each other.

"The saloon," Parker said.

***

Clint knew that going into the Golden Nugget would announce he was back in town. And why would he be back? Big Jack would have to surmise it was because he started working the Diamond mine, leaving no doubt that he had done something to Benny Diamond.

"If Foreman's not in here—" Parker said.

"There's another saloon," Clint said, "one the miners don't use. Let's not jump to conclusions and assume Foreman's also missing, now."

"If he is," Parker said, "I ain't gonna wait. I'm gonna put a bullet between Big Jack's eyes."

"That'll force the sheriff's hand," Clint said. "He'll have to enforce the law."

"I'll put a bullet in him, too," Parker said. "Remember, I'm already on the wrong side of the law."

"Butch," Clint said, "let's take it a step at a time."

"You know Big Jack killed your friend Diamond," Parker said. "He must've."

"If he did," Clint said, "I'll be with you."

They went through the batwing doors.

***

The result of Clint and Parker entering the Golden Nugget Saloon was almost immediate. At the bar John York elbowed Big Jack Hunter, who turned and looked. The other miners in the Nugget fell silent; the place got very quiet. Dixie and Jackie were among the crowd, and they stopped and stared, as well.

"What the hell—" Big Jack said.

***

Clint looked over at Big Jack and didn't have to approach him to speak and be heard in the quiet saloon.

"Didn't expect me back so soon, did you?" he asked.

"I didn't expect ya back at all," Big Jack said. "And I advise you to turn around and ride out, again."

"Where's Foreman?" Parker asked.

"Who?" Big Jack asked.

"If I don't find 'im," Parker went on, "you're a dead man."

Big Jack spread his arms.

"You're talkin' big, for someone who's in a room full of miners."

"I don't care how many miners you got behind ya," Parker said. "I'll kill you first, and you'll never see what happens after that."

Big Jack decided to ignore Parker and looked at Clint.

"Why're you back?" he demanded.

"This is why."

Clint took out the chunk of ore, which was the size of a kid's ball, and tossed it at Big Jack, who managed to catch it before it hit him in the face.

"That came out of Benny Diamond's mine," Clint said. "If you don't produce Benny, alive and well, my bullet will go into your skull right next to Butch's, here. That's two bullets in your head, Big Jack. Then the other miners can do what they want, but you'll be dead. You've got until tomorrow morning for us to see Benny and Foreman, alive."

Clint and Parker both backed carefully out the bat-wing doors.

Once outside Clint said, "Come on, we got one more saloon to check."

Chapter Forty

Clint hadn't been back to the second saloon since his first time there. As he entered, he saw the same three men seated in the same positions. The bartender, still looking bored, stood up straight.

"I heard you left town," he said.

"I came back," Clint said, as he and Parker approached the bar. "Two beers."

"Foreman ain't here," Parker said, "I feel like goin' back to the Nugget and takin' care of Big Jack."

"I gave him til mornin'," Clint said. "Let's stick to that."

"What if nothin' changes by then?"

"One thing will," Clint said.

"What?"

"He won't have every miner in town behind him."

The bartender set down the two beers.

"Ever find Benny?" he asked.

"No," Clint said, "and now we've lost another man." He described Foreman.

"Ain't seen anybody like that," the bartender said.

"You've got a lot of patience," Parker said to Clint. "How d'ya do that?"

"I don't use my gun unless I know there's no other way," Clint said.

"And are we there yet?" the younger man asked.

"We will be tomorrow morning."

"If we get to mornin'," Parker said. "What's to stop those miners from comin' at us tonight?"

"We are," Clint said. "We're going to stay in one room and watch each other's back all night. To tell you the truth, I wouldn't mind if they made a try for us. It'd make everything we do after that self-defense."

"You know," Parker said, "you ain't the man your reputation says you are."

"Most reputations are blown out of proportion, Butch," Clint told him.

"Well," Parker said, "I'm gonna make sure that Butch Cassidy's reputation is well earned. And this town's gonna find out just who I am."

Clint could see the fire in the young man's eyes and was pretty sure the time was going to come when he couldn't control the youngster, at all.

***

"Whiskey," Big Jack said to the bartender.

"You sure?" the bartender asked. "You don't usually drink whiskey."

"Just pour!"

The bartender poured and Big Jack knocked it back.

"What do we do now?" John York asked.

"I'm tempted," Big Jack said, "to try and take care of the Gunsmith tonight."

"How? Stormin' his hotel? We might lose a few," York said.

So far Big Jack had been able to use his miners to get what he wanted without losing any men.

"We'll wait, then," Big Jack said. "We don't want to give Adams the chance to claim self-defense."

"So you're gonna wait until he comes after you?" York asked.

"I think," Big Jack said, "we're gonna let him come up the mountain after us."

"Us?" York asked.

Big Jack looked at the bartender and said, "Two whiskeys."

Chapter Forty-One

Clint and Parker got very little sleep, and spent much of the time playing cards, trying to stay alert. At one point Parker did doze off, and when he jerked awake he saw Clint watching him.

"You get any sleep, at all?" he asked.

"None," Clint said. "Somebody had to stay on watch."

"Sorry," Parker said, rubbing his face.

"No problem," Clint said, "I couldn't sleep, anyway."

"Did you even hear anythin' in the hall?" Parker asked.

"No, not a sound," Clint said. "I think Big Jack might be smarter than we thought. He's not going to allow us to claim self-defense."

"Then we have to go after him."

"Yes," Clint said, "and that means going up the mountain."

"Right into his back yard."

"Exactly," Clint said, "but after breakfast let's check Foreman's room one more time."

They walked down the hall and entered Foreman's room. There was no indication that he had been there since they last checked. His saddlebags were still in a corner, along with his rifle.

"He wouldn't leave without those," Parker said.

"That means whenever he left the room, he intended to come back."

"If he's still alive, we ain't got time for breakfast," Parker said. "We gotta get up to Big Jack's camp."

"If he's holding Foreman, it won't be at his own camp."

"Then where?"

"Butch, let's go and have some breakfast," Clint said, "and we can talk about it. We can't go running up there, half-cocked."

"Yeah, okay," Parker said, "I *am* hungry."

"So am I."

***

"Back again," the waiter said.

"Couldn't stay away," Clint said. "Bacon-and-eggs for both of us."

"That's all?"

"And coffee," Clint said. "That's all. Thanks."

The waiter nodded and withdrew. There were no other diners in the place. They waited until they had been served their food, and the waiter returned to the kitchen to start talking again.

"When you went up there and grabbed that chunk of ore," Clint said, "did you see how many men were working the Diamond mine?"

"I saw three goin' in and out," Parker said. "That don't mean there weren't more inside, but I only saw three."

"I think maybe we should start there," Clint said. "If we're only facing three miners, we should be able to get the upper hand."

"And then what?"

"And then find out what they know," Clint said. "They might tell us something helpful about Benny, or Foreman."

"So I might get to use my gun?" Parker asked.

"You might," Clint said, "but here's how I'd like you to use it . . ."

***

After breakfast they walked to the base of the mountain.

"I thought gold was mined using water," Parker said.

"Sometimes it is," Clint said. "They use panning or sluicing, but what we have here, Butch, is hard rock mining. Rather than getting the gold out of sediment, it has to be dug out of the rock."

"Like the piece I took."

"Exactly. Now let's go up and hope they're so busy digging it out that they don't notice us until it's too late."

They started up the path.

***

Inside the Diamond mine, Eddie and his two men were busy with their pickaxes, chipping rock from the walls and depositing it into a wheelbarrow. When Eddie turned the barrow to walk out, he saw Clint Adams and Butch Cassidy standing there, the younger man with his gun in his hand.

"What the hell—" Eddie said.

The other men turned to see what he was cursing at.

"Drop the pickaxes, boys," Clint ordered, and they obeyed, their eyes wide.

"Keep coming," Clint said to Eddie, "and bring your two men with you."

Clint and Parker backed out, followed by the three miners, Eddie still pushing the wheelbarrow.

"Okay, set the wheelbarrow down," Clint said, when they were all outside. "We're going to have a little talk, gents, and if you don't tell us what we want to know, my friend Butch, here, is going to get to use his gun."

All three men looked at Butch, who smiled.

Chapter Forty-Two

"Are you in charge?" Clint asked.

"Uh, yeah."

"What's your name?"

"Eddie Granger."

"Where's Benny, Eddie?" Clint asked.

"I, uh, I dunno."

The other two men were eyeing Butch's gun nervously. Clint wasn't even thinking of him as Robert Leroy Parker anymore, he was Butch Cassidy.

"Do either of you know where Benny Diamond is?" Clint asked. He didn't care what their names were.

"I don't," one said.

"No, idea," the other said.

"But you're working his mine," Clint said.

"We're just doin' what we're told," the first miner said.

"By who?" Clint asked.

They both pointed and one of them said, "Eddie."

"Butch," Clint said, "take these two over there and see what you can find out. If you're not satisfied, shoot them both."

"Wha—" one started, but Butch cut him off.

"Let's go!" He gestured with his gun, and they all walked away, far enough so that Clint couldn't hear what was being said, and neither could they.

"Jesus," Eddie said, "are you gonna kill us?"

"Could be," Clint said. "I'm kind of fed up with looking for Benny and not finding him. You know who I am, right?"

"Y-yeah," Eddie said, "you're the Gunsmith."

"I assume you're afraid of your boss, Big Jack."

"Hell, yeah," Eddie said. "Everybody on this mountain is afraid of Big Jack."

"Was Benny Diamond afraid of him?"

"No."

"Look, friend," Clint said, drawing his gun and jamming the barrel into the miner's stomach, "I think you're going to have to be more afraid of me than you are of Big Jack. What do you think?"

"Y-yessir!"

"Did Big Jack kill, or have somebody kill, Benny Diamond?" Clint asked.

"I—I think so," Eddie said, "but I don't know for sure. Honest!"

"If Big Jack had somebody kill him, who would it have been?"

"H-he usually gives those kinds of jobs to York, John York."

"Is York a miner?"

"Yeah, but he don't spend so much time in the mines, if ya know what I mean."

"He does other kinds of jobs for Jack."

"Y-yeah."

So chances were good this John York had killed Benny Diamond.

"Where would York be now?" Clint asked.

"A-at Big Jack's camp," Eddie said. "Th-they said they . . ."

"They said what?"

"They said they was gonna wait there for you to come to them," Eddie told him.

That sounded like the truth to Clint.

"I've got one more question for you, Eddie," Clint said. "If you live or die depends on whether or not I like the answer."

"O-okay."

"Where's Earl Foreman?"

"I—I don't know who t-that is," Eddie said, his eyes going glassy as he stared at Clint's gun.

Clint kept the gun buried in the man's belly for a few seconds longer, then removed and holstered it.

"I'm going to believe what you've told me, Eddie," Clint said, "but if I find out you've been lying—"

"I ain't lied!" Eddie gasped out. "I ain't, only . . ."

"Only what?"

"Only d-don't tell Big Jack what I tol' ya."

Clint slapped the man lightly on the cheek and said, "It'll be our little secret, Eddie."

***

Butch came back over with the other two men and told Clint, "They don't know much, but they said Big Jack's waitin' in his camp for us."

"Anything else?"

"They said a man named John York is the one Big Jack gave the messy jobs to," Butch said, "like killin' somebody."

"That's what I got from Eddie, too," Clint said.

"So what now?"

"Let's get these three trussed up tight and stick them in the mine," Clint said. "And then we just keep going up."

Chapter Forty-Three

They started up the mountain toward Big Jack's camp, but before they got there, something occurred to Clint, and he stopped walking.

"What is it?"

"If Big Jack killed Benny, it was to get his mine."

"So?"

"So why would he kill Earl?" Clint asked. "He doesn't even know him."

"So you think Earl's still alive."

"I do."

"Then where is he?"

"I don't think Big Jack would keep him at his own camp," Clint said, "but there's two other mines he's taken over."

"Graham's Acre," Butch said, "and Anton Dowler's."

"Right," Clint said. "And they're on the way to Jack's camp."

"So we're gonna check them, first?"

"That's what we're going to do, Butch," Clint said. "That's exactly what we're going to do.

***

They reached Graham's Acre and found the man working the mine alone.

"What kin I do for ya?" Stevens asked.

"We need to look around, Graham," Clint said. "That's all."

"Well, go ahead," Stevens said. "Ain't nothin' here."

They went into the mine and had a look. Turned out the man was right. There was nothing to see.

"Whataya lookin' fer?" Stevens asked.

"Not what?" Clint said. "Who? Is Dowler up at his mine?"

"Ain't seen him come down," Stevens said.

"Anybody up there with him?" Clint asked.

"Not that I know of."

"If we find any surprises," Clint said, "we'll be back."

"I ain't goin' nowhere."

Clint and Parker continued up the mountain until they were approaching Anton Dowler's operation.

"Let's go slow," Clint said. "We don't know how many miners are working this claim. I think it's only Dowler, but we can't be sure."

When they reached the camp, they held back and watched. Finally, enough time passed where they thought they had their answer. Anton Dowler was alone, going in-and-out of the mine.

"Okay," Clint said, "I'm satisfied he's alone. Let's go."

They approached the mouth of the mine as Dowler went back in, so that when he came out, he'd find them waiting for him.

"What's this?" he asked.

"This is where you stay out here with Butch while I go inside and have a look."

Dowler didn't say anything, just stepped aside.

Clint went inside, followed the path lit by lamp hanging on the mine walls. There were tools strewn about and a wheelbarrow in a corner. He was about to go past when he thought he saw something behind the wheelbarrow. As he got closer, he saw a blanket that seemed to be covering a figure. He walked over to it, took hold of a corner, and pulled the blanket away, expecting to find a dead body, possibly Benny Diamond's. Instead, he found a very much alive Earl Foreman, bruised, bound and gagged.

He pulled the blanket completely off as Foreman looked up at him.

"I got you, Earl," he said, turning the man so he could untie him and remove the gag. "Butch is going to be very happy to see you."

"I'm afraid there's somethin' you ain't gonna be happy to see, Adams," Foreman said.

"What's that?"

"This way."

Foreman led Clint to another part of the mine, deeper in, where there was another blanket-covered figure.

"Damn," Clint said. "Is that . . ."

". . . your friend, Benny Diamond," Foreman said. "He's wrapped up tight and I think they sprinkled him with something to keep the stench down until they can figure out how to dispose of him."

"And you?" Clint asked. "What happened? And why are you still alive?"

"I left my room to get a drink, ran into some miners in the Golden Nugget. One of them was named York."

"Big Jack's right hand man," Clint said. "I'm pretty sure he killed Benny. The question is, why didn't he kill you?"

"I made the mistake of opening my big mouth, and the miner's took offense. But York didn't check with Big Jack first before he dragged me up here and left me. I figured once he checked with Jack on what to do, he'd be back, and I'd be dead. When you pulled the blanket off me, I thought it was him, and that was it."

"Well," Clint said, "it wasn't him, Foreman, but this *is* it. Come on, Butch is waiting outside."

Chapter Forty-Four

They tied Anton Dowler up and put him in the mine where Foreman had been. Even if York or Big Jack managed to get there, when they saw the blanketed figure, they'd still think it was Foreman. But Clint was determined to end things before that could happen.

They found a rifle that belonged to Dowler and gave it to Foreman.

"You feelin' up to this, Earl?" Butch asked.

"Oh yeah," Foreman said. "I wanna get these bastards. They were gonna kill me. And they killed Benny Diamond."

"All right, then," Clint said. "We're going to go the rest of the way up to Big Jack Hunter's mine. We want Hunter, and we want York."

"Right," Foreman said.

"I don't know which one is York," Butch said.

"Earl and I will point him, out," Clint said, "and we all know what Big Jack looks like."

"Then let's finally get this done" Butch said, "so we can all get the hell out of this town."

***

"You did what?" Big Jack asked.

"He was runnin' his mouth and threatenin' us," York said. "What were we supposed to do?"

"Where is he?" Jack asked.

"He's in Anton's mine, where we left Benny," York said.

"John, did you kill 'im?" Jack asked.

"I wouldn't do that without checkin' with you first, Jack," York said.

"Well, now you've checked," Jack said. "Go and kill 'im."

"And then what do we do with 'im?" York asked.

"The same thing you did with Benny," Jack said. "And when Adams is gone, we'll get rid of both bodies. Now get to it. Take two men with you."

"Right," York said. "I'll take Eddie and Nick."

Jack knew who Eddie was. There were plenty of other men whose names he didn't know.

"Whoever," he said. "Just get it done and then come back here. I'm gonna need you when we take care of Adams."

"Got it."

York turned and went in search of Eddie and Nick.

***

"Hunter's claim is just up ahead," Clint said.

"Good," Foreman said. "Maybe we can get off this ledge. I almost fell off this damn mountain twice."

The path, as they went higher, got more narrow. Not so narrow that they might fall, but he apparently had a problem with heights. The first time he slipped, they decided he should walk behind Clint and in front of Butch. He slipped only one time after that, almost dropping the rifle.

Now they could hear voices ahead of them, signaling them they were close to the camp.

"Don't shoot unless I do," Clint told them. "Got it?"

"We got it, Clint," Butch said.

They continued on and came into the clearing of the camp, when Foreman found much wider and easier footing. He breathed a sigh of relief.

The miner's in the camp turned and looked at them. There were probably eight or ten, but none were armed, except for their shovels and pickaxes.

Clint saw York standing with two men, one he knew as Eddie. York was the only man with a gun, which was tucked into his belt.

"Everybody just stand still," Clint ordered. "We're looking for York, and Big Jack."

"Whataya want me for?" York asked.

"Well," Clint said, "you kidnapped this man and left him in Anton Dowler's mine—along with the body of Benny Diamond. I assume you killed Benny and were probably on your way to kill Foreman."

"I didn't kill anybody," York said, "and I tied him up because he was askin' for it."

"And what's Benny's body doing in the mine?" Clint asked.

"Whataya askin' me for? You should be asking Anton. It's his mine."

"Before we tied and gagged Anton, he confirmed that you and some other men brought Benny's body to his mine, and then brought Foreman."

"You're not in friendly territory, Adams," York told him. "There are more than a dozen miners here, and they're not armed. But that doesn't mean they can't do a lot of damage."

"We've got more than twelve bullets, York," Clint told him.

"You can't shoot unarmed men," York said.

"But they're not unarmed," Clint said. "I see shovels and pickaxes, which in the hands of men who know how to use them, are weapons. And you have a gun. So we won't have any problem shooting any of you."

The miners began to exchange glances, and some of them even put their tools down.

"Now," Clint asked, "Where's Big Jack?"

Chapter Forty-Five

York looked around at the miners, who reacted by picking their tools up again.

"Get ready," Clint said to Butch and Foreman. "They're afraid of Big Jack, and probably York, as well. "If they charge us, we'll have to fire."

"I can't wait," Butch said.

"Don't fire," Clint said. "I'm going to try something."

Clint drew and fired three times, quickly, at three men who were holding pickaxes. When he was a done, they were simply holding axe handles. The heads had been cleanly shot off and were lying on the ground. Then he quickly reloaded while the miners stared.

"Holy—" one miner said, and all the others simply dropped their shovels and axes.

York knew he had no choice. His only chance was to draw his gun and fire while the Gunsmith was reloading. But as he went for his weapon, Butch saw what was happening and reacted. He drew his gun, fired once, hitting York in the chest. The man staggered back several steps before sinking to his knees and then falling on his face in the dirt.

Clint looked at Butch, then down at York's body, and the gun next to it.

"Thanks," he said to Butch.

"Don't mention it."

The miners were also staring down at York's body, and Clint decided to take control.

"That's it, it's all over," Clint said. "Any miner who picks up a shovel or an axe to do anything but take it into the mine is a dead man."

The tools were staying in the dirt for the foreseeable future.

"Now where's Big Jack?"

Eddie stepped forward and said, "He should be in his shack, Mr. Adams."

Clint turned to Butch and Foreman.

"You two watch these men while I check."

"Got it," Butch said, and Foreman raised his rifle to cover the miners.

Clint walked across the clearing to the shack, where he had slept one night. The flimsy door was unlocked, so he flung it open and darted inside.

There was no sign of Big Jack.

Clint came out of the shack and looked at the miners. The only one who actually knew where Big Jack was, was probably on the ground, dead.

Clint decided to key on the one called Eddie.

"You," he said, pointing, "come here."

"Me?" Eddie asked.

"Yes, you," Clint said, impatiently. "Come here."

Eddie walked over and stood in front of Clint, near the shack.

"If Big Jack's not in there, where would he be?" Clint asked.

"Geez, I dunno—"

"I'm not in the mood for lies, Eddie," Clint said. "Tell me what you *do* know."

"If-if he ain't in his shack, and he ain't in the mine," Eddie said, "he might be in town."

Clint looked at Butch.

"I'll check the mine," Butch said, while Foreman continued to keep the miners covered. Butch went in and quickly came back out. "He ain't in there."

Clint looked at Eddie.

"How could he have gotten past us to go back to town?"

"T-there's another way down," Eddie said, "but it's kind of steep."

Clint looked at Butch.

"You and Earl go down the way we came up," Clint said. "I'm going to have Eddie take me down the other way."

"Clint," Butch said, "don't fall off this mountain."

"I'll do my best," Clint said.

Chapter Forty-Six

Eddie had been telling the truth.

The alternate route down the mountain was very steep, indeed. Clint had to holster his gun and make sure it wouldn't slip during the descent. He also had to keep Eddie in front of him, so there was no chance of the man somehow knocking him off the mountain.

It was a path, but it was the kind you had to be a mountain goat to traverse. Certain foot and handholds had to be used, but eventually they got to the bottom. Clint kept a wary eye on Eddie, in case the man decided to run as soon as his feet touched flat ground. But that turned out not to be the case.

"You ain't gonna kill me, are ya?" Eddie asked, when they reached the bottom.

"No, Eddie, I'm not," Clint said. "Where do you think Big Jack would go?"

"If he's waitin' to hear that York killed you, probably the saloon," Eddie said.

"All right," Clint said, "let's go and check the Golden Nugget. If he's there, I'll let you go."

***

Clint had to give Big Jack Hunter credit. The man wasn't hiding. The saloon was about half-filled with locals, as the miners were still on the mountain. But seated alone, right in the center of the room, was Big Jack. Because of the size of him, he stood out.

"He's here!" Eddie said, with relief, as they both peered over the batwing doors.

Clint looked at Eddie and said, "You can go, Eddie."

"Thanks, Mr. Adams!" Eddie said. "Watch out for him, though. He's a tricky bastard."

"Thanks for the warning," Clint said, and entered the saloon.

Big Jack had a half-filled beer mug in front of him, with an empty shot glass next to it. Clint went to the bar ordered two more beers.

"You joinin' Big Jack?" the man asked.

"You could say that."

"I'd be careful if I was you," the bartender said. "He's been drinkin' whiskey. He hardly ever drinks whiskey. It . . . does somethin' to him."

"Thanks for the warning."

Clint carried the two full mugs over to Big Jack's table.

"Mind if I join you?"

"That depends," Big Jack said. "Is York dead?"

"He is."

"You kill 'im?"

"Actually, no, young Butch did."

"Ah. Is one of those for me?"

Clint put a beer down in front of Big Jack.

"Have a seat," the miner said.

Clint sat across from the big man, saw that his eyes were red with an alcoholic haze.

"I also found Foreman, and Benny."

"Poor Benny," Big Jack said. "He didn't leave me much of a choice. Unlike Graham Stevens and Anton Dowler, he wouldn't sign his claim over to me."

"So you took it."

"Yes."

"By killing him."

"Well . . . York killed him."

"On your orders."

Big Jack took a drink.

"Come on, Jack," Clint said, "York didn't kill without your say-so. That's why Foreman's still alive."

"I never told York to touch Foreman," Big Jack said. "That was just a stupid mistake."

"I don't think York's the only one who made stupid mistakes," Clint said.

"Look," Jack said, "I did what I did, and I ain't gonna apologize for it. If you wanna kill me for it, go ahead." He spread his arms. "I'm unarmed."

Clint thought that a man that size, with arms like tree trunks, could never be considered unarmed. In spite of the two warnings he had received—from Eddie and the bartender—he was still surprised when Big Jack overturned the table on him in a drunken rage.

Clint went over backwards in his chair, but at the same time he drew his gun. As Big Jack closed in on him, huge hands reaching for him, he pointed the gun.

"Jack—"

The big miner's hand swatted the gun away. It flew from Clint's hand, across the room and landed at the base of the bar.

His eyes on fire, Big Jack grabbed ahold of the front of Clint's shirt and yanked him to his feet. Then those big hands closed around Clint's neck.

At that point Butch and Earl Foreman came through the batwing doors. The other patrons of the saloon had gotten to their feet, watching the action. Nobody was making a move to help Clint.

"Jesus," Foreman said, raising the rifle.

"Wait," Butch said, "give Clint a chance."

"Jack's gonna crush 'im!" Foreman said.

"He's the Gunsmith, Earl," Butch reminded him. "Watch."

Clint knew there was no way he could match Big Jack's strength. The only way to fight a man like that—in a ring, or in a saloon—was dirty.

He brought his knee up into Jack's groin. When there was no reaction, he did it again, as hard as he could. Big Jack roared in pain and tossed Clint aside. He landed, slid across the floor and came to a stop at the base of the bar. As Big Jack started for him again, he picked his gun up off the floor and shot him.

Three times . . .

***

"Self-defense," Clint said.

Sheriff Bates Monroe stared at Clint for a few moments.

"Isn't that what they said?" Clint asked.

"That's what everybody said last night," Monroe answered. "If you hadn't shot 'im, he would've killed you with his bare hands."

"Right. So what are you going to do?"

"I suppose I could arrest you, hold you for trial so everybody who was in the saloon last night would have to testify, but what's the point? Besides, we don't even have a jail." The sometime lawman leaned on his pitchfork. "I guess you'll be leavin' town."

"As soon as I make sure Benny Diamond was properly buried," Clint said, and walked his Tobiano outside, where he found Butch Cassidy and Earl Foreman on their horses.

"So guess he's not gonna act like a lawman," Butch said.

"He hasn't so far," Clint said, "why start now?"

"Mind if we ride part way with you?" Butch asked.

"I don't mind at all, Butch."

Author's Note

It was a few years later Butch Cassidy robbed his first bank, and it just happened to be the San Miguel Bank in Columbia, which is now called Telluride, Colorado. Still later, he went on to form The Wild Bunch, which included Harry Alonzo Longabaugh, also known as "The Sundance Kid."

Photo and/or Image Credit

commons.wikimedia.org/wiki/File:Butch_Cassidy.jpg by Fernando de Gorocica wikidata.org/wiki/Special:CentralAuth?target=Fernando+de+Gorocica is licensed under creativecommons.org/licenses/by/2.0/

Coming February 27, 2021

THE GUNSMITH

467

The Lady Sheriff

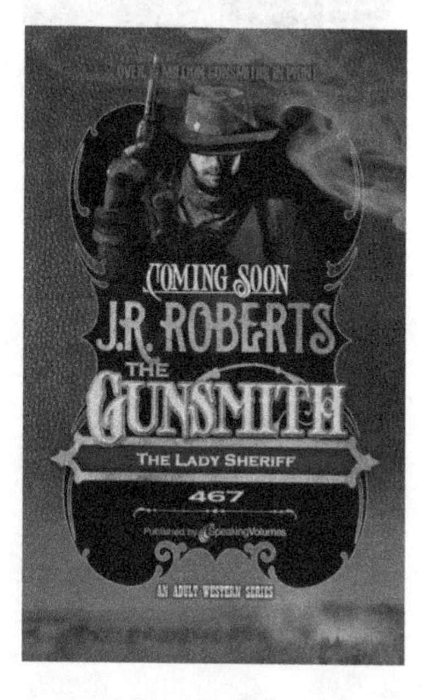

For more information
visit: www.SpeakingVolumes.us

On Sale Now!

Award-Winning Author
Robert J. Randisi (J.R. Roberts)

For more information
visit: www.SpeakingVolumes.us

CPSIA information can be obtained
at www.ICGtesting.com
Printed in the USA
LVHW031729180521
687788LV00005B/267